TURN TWO
by Nancy Warren

"Why are you here, Taylor?"

"Because I got offered a great job."

"There are jobs all over the country. Even in Australia, I bet."

"You can't imagine that I took this job because you were here?"

"That unlikely but flattering possibility had crossed my mind. How'd you find out about the job? I doubt it was posted in the *Sydney Herald.*"

"No. Of course not. Reena e-mailed me. She had an opening for a PR manager."

"I see."

"Reena must have known you were here.   But she never breathed a word to me."

"I'm detecting some matchmaking here."

"Matchmaking? What is she, crazy? We hate each other."

"Be careful with the word *we.* I've got divorce papers that stipulate there is no *we.*" Mike leaned forward, uncrossing his arms. "And you have no idea what I feel about you."

Dear Reader,

I'd already written *Speed Dating,* my first book in Harlequin's officially licensed NASCAR series, when I came across a little item in the *Charlotte Observer* by columnist Jeff Elder, who sadly noted that *Speed Dating* contained no balding columnist. And right then my new hero was born. Okay, he is *not* bald, but Mike Lundquist is otherwise a lot like Jeff. Sweet, smart, funny and very sexy in his own way. When I told Jeff I was making my new hero a columnist, he took on the task of introducing me to Charlotte as an insider. Thanks for our date in Charlotte, Jeff.

I'm also immensely grateful to Jamie Rodway of Roush Racing, who is one of my favorite people in racing and who spent a couple of hours in a hotel lobby in Daytona answering my newbie questions. I'm also grateful to Lisa Schmitz, Raygan from NASCAR.com, David Poole of the *Charlotte Observer* and Angie Skinner, who wrote a fun NASCAR cookbook and kindly told me all about her wedding to driver Mike Skinner. Thanks as always to Marsha Zinberg, Michelle Renaud and Melissa Gawalko.

Finally, thanks to Carl Edwards, who is my favorite NASCAR driver and all around good guy, to everyone at Roush and to the wonderful women of the NASCAR Library Collection.

Happy reading,

Nancy

NASCAR

TURN TWO

Nancy Warren

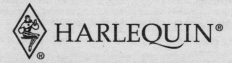

HARLEQUIN®

TORONTO • NEW YORK • LONDON
AMSTERDAM • PARIS • SYDNEY • HAMBURG
STOCKHOLM • ATHENS • TOKYO • MILAN • MADRID
PRAGUE • WARSAW • BUDAPEST • AUCKLAND

ISBN-13: 978-0-373-21783-0
ISBN-10:   0-373-21783-8

TURN TWO

NANCY WARREN

is a *USA TODAY* bestselling author of more than thirty romantic novels and novellas. She has won numerous awards for her writing and in 2004 was a double finalist for the prestigious RITA® Award. Nancy lives in the Pacific Northwest, where she includes among her hobbies a growing fixation with the NASCAR channel. For more on Nancy, her releases, writing tips and background visit her on the Web at www.nancywarren.net.

This book is dedicated to two wonderful writing friends,
Kathleen Shandley and Bobby Hutchinson.
Thanks for everything.

CHAPTER ONE

Taylor Robinson had envisioned countless scenarios that could ruin her first day on the job as the public relations manager for a rookie NASCAR driver. She had extra panty hose in her bag, an EpiPen in case some new and hitherto unknown allergic reaction should try to fell her on her first day; she had her makeup bag, a few hair products, a tiny sewing kit, even extra shoes in case she should snap a heel.

But not her worst nightmare—and she was an imaginative woman—could have prepared her for running into the one man she'd planned never to see again.

Her ex-husband.

The day started out promisingly enough.

She entered Winfield Racing headquarters near Charlotte, North Carolina, and was immediately greeted by Reena Boscoff, account manager for Winfield Racing and an old family friend who had tracked Taylor down in Australia to offer her the PR job.

After a rib-bruising hug, Reena said, "Okay, I'm

swamped. We'll catch up later. Here's Hank Mission's schedule."

Taylor blinked back the jet lag and focused on the computer printout. "Is this event this afternoon?"

Reena put on her reading glasses and peered at the printout. "Yep. Rookie of the Year event. Three o'clock today." She let her glasses slip back so they hung from a gold chain around her neck. "Good thing I had your business cards printed in advance. Come on. I'll introduce you to your driver."

And poof, any thoughts of easing into her new job were gone.

Six hours later Taylor walked into one of the big kickoff events for the upcoming season. She realized she'd forgotten one important item in her emergency pack. Beta-blockers. After thirteen months on surfing beaches, she wasn't sure she could handle this much stress in one day.

The usual noises of a social event in full swing hit Taylor as she entered the hotel ballroom with Hank Mission, Winfield's rookie driver, and Dylan Hargreave, Winfield's senior driver.

A country band was playing, a lot of people talking and laughing, probably seeing one another for the first time in months. At one end a stage area was set up for the media event, but for now the atmosphere had more in common with a cocktail party than a press conference.

She recognized a couple of famous racing faces, but most of the people present were strangers.

They walked deeper into the crowded room, and Dylan was soon swapping greetings in a casual, practiced manner as they made their way forward. Hank tended to hang back a little and obviously didn't know many more people here than she did.

Hank was twenty-five years old and hailed from a small town in South Carolina, and he had the accent to prove it. He was medium height with a flop of brown hair and a crooked grin. He came across as shy, but there was a certain expression in his eyes that hinted at devilry. She liked him immediately, which was a good thing considering that looking after him was going to be her full-time job.

She shook hands when introduced, made a point of handing out the new business cards and felt her old reporter's instincts resurface.

Taylor wasn't one to let the grass grow. Maybe she'd only been back in the country three days, still felt like she had sand between her toes and a persistent case of jet lag, but she planned to raise the profile of her driver starting today.

"Jeff," she said to Dylan's PR manager, figuring he'd be an expert on the subject, "who are the media people I really need to know?"

Checking first to see that his driver was happily chatting to Hank and one of the event organizers, Jeff pointed out a bubbly young blond woman who worked for an online publication and then a spotlessly groomed broadcaster, telling her a bit about each. She wished she could pull out a reporter's notebook and write it all down. Instead she concentrated, trying to memorize everything Jeff told her.

"And over there is the man whose racing column has become the single most significant source of racing news."

Her gaze followed Jeff's.

And then snagged on a most unwelcome sight.

Her breath caught.

"Mike Lundquist," she blurted in the tone she might have used if Freddy Krueger was eyeing her from across the room.

"That's right," Jeff said, as though she'd answered a skill-testing question correctly. "Somebody's been doing their homework."

Mike Lundquist was the man she'd been married to for three years. The man she'd gone halfway around the world to forget.

His hair was the color of dark chocolate, his eyes even darker. He had round cheeks, weighed ten pounds more than he should, and had a humorous grin that was, as she knew too well, a chick magnet. He wasn't movie-star handsome, yet he drew people to him with a combination of charm and easy humor.

The sight of him across a crowded, noisy ballroom had her churning with a mixture of emotions so confused she couldn't begin to separate them.

"A year ago nobody'd heard of the guy, now his is the most trusted voice in racing."

"Mike Lundquist is the most trusted voice in

NASCAR?" This could not be happening. He was supposed to be in Seattle, far, far away from here.

"Yep. He's got a syndicated racing column that everybody reads. If you can get on his good side, Hank's halfway to fame and glory."

She felt like there wasn't enough air in the ballroom. Heck, in all of North Carolina. If Jeff was to be believed, her ex-husband was the one man she most needed to impress if she wanted to succeed at her job.

She wished, quite fervently, that she hadn't signed that six-month lease on her apartment, because it looked like she'd be moving on again faster than you can say "Irreconcilable differences."

Mike was leaning over a table, talking to a woman. He was describing something with his hands. It was so familiar to watch those hands emphasizing his words that her stomach jolted. She'd known she didn't want to see him again, but she'd had no idea how badly. The worst part was that he still looked the same. He wore his dark brown hair longer than she remembered, but otherwise he was unchanged.

He wore a brown corduroy jacket and a plaid shirt, and she knew without looking that he wore jeans and loafers.

It had been so long since she'd seen him that she couldn't seem to stop staring. The woman he was telling the story to was obviously enjoying it. Even from here Taylor could see her leaning forward to catch every word, laughing and nodding.

Then an odd thing happened. His hands stopped moving and he raised his head, slowly, like the Terminator when he senses his prey is near. It couldn't be possible that her ex-husband would sense her presence, but she saw his gaze begin to sweep the room.

Naturally, she did the sensible, mature thing.

She dove out of sight behind the first body she could find.

CHAPTER TWO

TAYLOR HAD ALMOST REGAINED her equilibrium—if an accelerated heart rate, adrenaline rushing like Niagara Falls and a flight response on overdrive could be called equilibrium—and had rejoined Dylan and Hank when Dylan gestured over her head, a grin splitting his face. She was about to turn when an odd shiver of premonition rolled up her spine.

"Hey," Dylan said, "Perfect timing. Taylor, right here is the guy you most need to impress in racing." He put a hand on the brown corduroy shoulder passing by and Taylor had half a second to prepare before her ex-husband said, "Hey, Dy. How's it going?"

Oh, God. Even his voice was the same. So exactly, frighteningly, the same.

"Good. Come meet Hank's new PR manager. Taylor Robinson."

Mike turned so sharply the beer in his glass sloshed over the rim. Their gazes met. She saw in that instant that he hadn't expected to see her any more than she'd expected to see him.

Light sprang into his eyes, and for a second everything fell away and she expected him to drag her into his arms and kiss her breathless. Her body leaned forward toward him and she felt a little dizzy.

His eyes were so dark. She'd always loved them. There was something serious and mysterious underneath the laughter that always seemed to sparkle on the surface.

Then the moment passed and all the stuff that was between them reared up as thick and prickly as a prison wall topped with barbed wire.

She felt hot and cold—and wanted this moment over so badly she couldn't breathe.

After a pause that seemed endless, but was probably less than two seconds, he spoke.

"Taylor." He extended his hand. "Good to meet you."

He was offering to shake her hand?

Another second or so passed.

In a slow-motion nightmare she saw her own hand reach out and shake that of her ex-husband. As though they hadn't shared a house, a bed and a car for three years. She'd imagined having grandchildren with this man. Now they were shaking hands like strangers. His touch was warm, so warm.

"Nice to meet you, too," she said, amazed at how normal she sounded.

His gaze stayed on hers even as his hand released her. "Taylor. That's an interesting name for a woman. Is it a family name?"

Oh, like he didn't know. "Yes." She smiled even though her lips felt stiff. "My mother's family name."

"And Robinson. Is that your maiden name? Or are you married?" He put a lazy emphasis on the word *maiden*.

"I'm not married," she snapped.

"You from Charlotte? I don't remember seeing you around before."

"No. I'm from out west." She narrowed her gaze at him slightly. And don't push it, she warned him silently.

"Taylor's been traveling," Hank said. "She was in Australia. Surfing."

"That would explain why your nose is peeling," Mike said, then turned to Dylan and asked him some technical question about spoilers that quickly went beyond Taylor's rudimentary understanding. Not that she could take in much of anything. She still felt stunned.

The conversation stayed on racing and she and Hank both stood silent. Dylan and Mike obviously had an easy, congenial relationship, one she hoped Hank would develop. Which would happen more easily if he had a different PR manager.

After five minutes or so, Mike turned to Hank. "Are you taking Taylor to Florida?"

What was she? A spare tire? An extra lug nut? They talked about her as if she could be transported in the hauler along with the engine parts.

"Naturally, I'll be traveling with the team," she said before Hank had a chance.

"Guess I'll see you in Daytona, then."

This bad cocktail party got worse and worse. "You travel the racing circuit?"

"It's easier to write a NASCAR column if I actually watch the races," he said, as though she weren't the brightest bulb in the package. Not that she could blame him. His presence had thrown her so she'd acted as inane as she had it in her to be.

Dylan waved, breaking into a huge grin, and an attractive, intelligent-looking woman with wide-spaced green eyes and a friendly smile walked up to join them. She wore a lightweight business suit in a coral color, and when she got close enough, Dylan caught her to him and kissed her, much the way Mike used to kiss Taylor when they were first married.

"Taylor, I'd like you to meet my fiancée, Kendall," Dylan said, interrupting her thoughts. "She's an actuary for an insurance company downtown. She walked over from her office."

"Part-time actuary," the woman corrected. "I travel to as many races as I can."

"Great to meet you," Taylor said, shaking hands. "And congratulations." She glanced automatically at Kendall's ring finger and was surprised to find it empty of any engagement ring. Maybe Kendall was a feminist. Taylor liked to think she was a feminist, too, but she didn't think she could turn down a couple of carats of sparkle to protest a patriarchal institution like marriage. "When's the wedding?"

"We haven't decided yet," Dylan said, fast, before Kendall could speak.

His fiancée sent him a glance of indulgent fondness. Taylor got the feeling that this woman knew exactly how her man ticked. "You make it sound like you don't want to marry me," she said to him. Although, from the way they looked at each other, anyone could see there was no hesitation going on there.

"Honey, you know that's not true," he said, sounding almost fierce.

Kendall turned back to Taylor. "We don't dare breathe a word about being engaged to anyone outside our close circle." Taylor had the odd experience of being suddenly an insider because of her position with Winfield Racing and Hank. "We want a low-key wedding and his mother and father want to make the Trump weddings look stingy."

Taylor blinked. "Could anyone do that?"

Kendall and Dylan shared a glance. "Dy's parents could."

"That must be kind of awkward," Taylor said.

"It will be fine. We just have to figure out a way to keep things secret so the wedding-planning troops can't be mobilized."

Taylor wondered how on earth a super successful NASCAR driver and one of *People*'s sexiest bachelors thought he was going to keep his wedding a secret. Unless he and Kendall eloped.

"You should elope," Mike said from beside her.

She was sipping her cola and nearly choked. "A lot of couples do it." She wouldn't look at him. She wouldn't. She'd kick him if she could get a good one in without anyone seeing.

"That's what Dylan says. He keeps trying to get me to elope to avoid the whole mess," Kendall said, "but this is the only wedding I plan to have, and I am going to enjoy it."

Taylor felt a blush warming her face. She knew without looking that Mike was gazing at her and his expression would be cynical.

"Good for you," she said, keeping her focus on the bride-to-be and ignoring as best she could the groom-that-was. Looking at the quiet, confident woman, Taylor had no doubt she'd get her wedding her way.

Seeing how Dylan's gaze lingered on Kendall's face as she spoke, Taylor imagined he knew it, too. He took her hand in his and they stood there, linked, a poster couple for true love, happily ever after and all that other stuff Taylor no longer believed in.

"Are you married, Taylor?" the other woman asked.

A pain, sharp and swift, twisted her heart. "No. No, I'm not."

"I never knew it could be this complicated."

You should try divorce, Taylor thought. The mean and tiny part of her adding, *And, statistically, there's a good chance you will.* No force on earth could stop her from glancing at her ex as the thought crossed her mind and she found his gaze on hers and knew how neatly he'd read her mind.

"Enough wedding talk. I swear I'm getting hives just thinking about it," Dylan said. "Mike, Hank here is looking great for the season." He chuckled as yet another gorgeous man joined their circle. "And here is the man who helped get him his ride. How's it going, Carl?"

"Great." Some women might get a thrill out of meeting Hugh Jackman or Dr. McDreamy. Taylor's knees went weak over NASCAR drivers, especially Carl Edwards, driver of the Number 99 car, who was her idea of Driver McDreamy with his sparkling blue eyes, strong chin and toothy grin, which he beamed her way when Dylan introduced them.

"Great to meet you, Taylor," he said.

"You, too," she managed to reply, hoping she sounded a lot cooler than she felt. For she'd made the shocking discovery that he was even better-looking in real life than he was on TV.

"You ready for this thing?" Carl asked Hank.

The Rookie of the Year event was a way of celebrating the new blood coming into the sport. Along with Hank, there were two other rookies in this year's race for the NASCAR NEXTEL Cup.

As a former Rookie of the Year himself, Carl, like Dylan, was here to say a few words to the new drivers.

"I hear there's a connection between you two," Mike said. He put his beer down on the table behind him and pulled out a reporter's notebook from his pocket.

Hank rocked back on his heels. "Yeah, there is. Carl's helped me out a lot."

"Walk me through it from the beginning, Hank. How'd you get started in racing?"

Mike would already know this stuff, of course. He followed the truck races, the Busch series and the NASCAR NEXTEL Cup Series, but he'd want to get Hank comfortable and maybe the young driver would say some things in his own words that would make good quotes.

She'd learned a lot about reporting from Mike when they'd worked together. Taylor had given up a promising career at the *Seattle Post Intelligencer* when, in the space of a few months, she lost her dad, her first pregnancy ended in a late miscarriage and her marriage disintegrated.

After running halfway around to world to escape her memories, it was almost too painful to watch her ex-husband working at what he did best.

Hank said, "I raced carts as a kid in South Carolina, then I got myself a late-model ride, went up to Missouri, raced once against Carl." He shrugged, looking modest, and she thought if they'd been standing on dirt or sand, he'd have kicked at it with his sneakers.

Carl picked up the story. "Hank was fearless." He laughed. "I remember thinking, 'I don't know who this guy is, but he's crazy.'" He glanced at Hank. "I mean, you were going all out. The last couple of laps were wild."

"Great race," Hank agreed.

"Who won?" Mike asked.

"Carl did," Hank quickly said.

"By half a car length," Carl said.

She liked them both for their modesty. Of course, she figured they'd always try to beat each other in a contest—any contest she suspected, from racing to dirt-biking to skipping rocks on a still lake. But when it came to talking about the race, neither was trying to one-up the other. It looked good on both of them.

"We got out at the end," Carl continued, "and I'm like, who is this guy? He's going places."

"Carl heard that Winfield had an opening and the next year I got a truck ride with Winfield Racing."

"How old were you?"

"Twenty. Spent a couple of years in trucks, a couple of years in Busch before I got my Cup ride."

Mike nodded. "How do you think you'll do this season?"

Hank grinned. "I've wanted to race in the NASCAR NEXTEL Cup Series ever since I can remember. I'm going to do the best I can is all I know."

"Okay. Good luck," Mike said, scribbling a final note and then flipping his notebook shut.

On stage they were getting ready for the formal part of the event, where the three rookies would be introduced. She walked Hank up to the stage area and stood to the side to watch. She thought Hank did very well, goofing around enough with the other two rookies that they made the event look like a lot of fun. Carl and Dylan acted like teachers, with pointers and chalkboards, while the rookie "students" sat in kid-size desks.

Cameras snapped, film rolled and pens and pencils scribbled. Somewhere among the scribblers was Mike Lundquist. She kept her gaze glued on Hank.

After the fun and the intros, Hank and Dylan walked together to where she and Jeff awaited them.

"You did great," she told Hank. "You made the event look like fun."

He looked at her as if she was crazy. "It *was* fun."

Oh, she thought, one part of her job was going to be a breeze. Hank was going to be a pleasure to work with.

Unlike certain people in the media.

CHAPTER THREE

"OKAY," DYLAN SAID. "LET'S DO some meeting and greeting and then head out of here."

"Oh, yeah, right," Hank replied. "Absolutely." He glanced toward the outdoors longingly, and they all laughed.

"Tell you what," Dylan said, "we'll move in a clockwise direction, make nice, introduce you and Taylor around, and then when we end up back here we'll sneak out and I'll take you out for barbecue."

"You're bribing me with food?" Hank asked, looking a lot less twitchy, Taylor noticed.

"Can you be bribed with food?"

That lightning grin lit the young driver's face. "Oh, yeah. Let's get to work."

For the next hour, she and Hank schmoozed like politicians in the primaries. She managed to meet most of the drivers who were there because, hey, they were her heroes, and why not? But she put her focus on introducing herself—and Hank—to the media, and several reporters did a quick interview with him on the spot.

She felt that Hank, as a rookie, was accorded interest more than respect. She suspected he'd have to earn that. Still, his quiet smile and self-deprecating manner made him easy to like. He had a good track record going into this first critical season and she felt certain that he was headed for a great career.

She soon had a fistful of business cards that she'd exchanged for her own. She scribbled a few notes on the back of each to help her remember who everybody was.

After downing a jet-lag-fighting cola, she excused herself to go to the washroom. When she returned, Hank was standing near the door with Dylan and Kendall. They'd completed the circuit and could leave, and she could head home and sleep.

Her heart sank when she realized the man standing with them was Mike. She'd worked the room always aware of his exact location as though she'd stuck a GPS device on him. Wherever he was, she made absolutely certain she wasn't. Now he was standing between her and her ride out of here.

She took a calming breath and walked over to join the group. As she did, she thought, here we are, Mike and her and NASCAR back together again. It was watching NASCAR races on rainy Seattle Sundays that had brought her and Mike together in the first place.

In a city not exactly famous for following NASCAR, she'd stuck out like a hitchhiker's thumb.

Now it seemed racing was bringing them back together whether she wanted a reunion or not.

"Taylor," Dylan said when she reached them, "you ready for some good barbecue? And I don't mean that 'put another shrimp on the barbie' stuff, I mean real Southern barbecue."

Kendall added, "It's on our way to drop you at your car if you'd rather get home." She smiled. "This must all be pretty overwhelming on your first day."

"It'd be fun if you came, though," Hank said.

Even as she opened her mouth to refuse, Mike said, challenge and taunting in his tone, "Yeah, Taylor. You coming?"

She was exhausted, her body clock still tuned to Queensland time, her brain almost exploding from all the new information she'd crammed in there today. She'd rather stick her own head down the garbage disposal in her apartment than spend another minute with Mike Lundquist. But he was going to be part of her life again, as much as she didn't want him to be, and they both might as well get used to it. She put on her best fake smile. "Sure. I'd love to come."

They piled into several vehicles. She was back with Dylan, Hank, Jeff and now Kendall. Mike brought his own car—a domestic compact that she didn't recognize. He'd got rid of their once-shared car, then. Two trucks pulled out behind them, and she hoped whoever was inside was also in the mood for barbecue. The more people there, the better.

Dylan took them to a big noisy place with huge

wooden rafters and a hopping bar attached to the restaurant. Fortunately, he'd drawn another half dozen
friends to join them.

Once she was seated between Hank and Kendall
she at least felt insulated from her ex. By an
unspoken arrangement, she and Mike were as far
apart from each other at the long table as it was
possible to get.

Most of the talk revolved around Daytona and the
upcoming season. Spirits were high. Everybody was
starting a fresh season and anything was possible.
They were a laughing, joking bunch, and Taylor
knew, but for one thing, she'd be thrilled with her
new job. That one thing was a big one, though. A
five-foot-eleven-inches, two-hundred-pound thing
who was the life of the party down at his end of the
table.

Ha, ha, ha, as if he didn't have a care in the world
or an ex-wife sitting a few seats down.

Okay, if he could do it, so could she. She turned
to Kendall. "Tell me all about yourself. And I'd be
grateful for any hints you've got on handling a
driver."

"You want hints on handling a driver, Taylor, you
should ask me," Hank said on her other side.

She turned to him, remembered something she'd
read in one of the articles about him.

"I hear you play practical jokes. I don't trust you."

He snorted with laughter and turned to tell Dylan
what she'd said.

"Hints on handling a driver," Kendall said, glancing fondly at Dylan. "Never let them have the upper hand. Accept that racing is tough on them emotionally and sometimes you need to be there to support them."

Hank was back to listening. "You forgot the kissing part, Kendall." He had a rib in one hand, and there was a smear of sauce on his chin as he turned to Taylor with a far-too-innocent look in his eyes. "Kendall turned Dy into a winner by kissing him before every race."

He'd spoken loud enough that the whole table could hear him.

"Not every woman's kisses bring luck, Hank," Mike said from the bottom of the table.

There was loud booing and Hank sent a hunk of bread flying down the table, which whacked her former husband in the general direction of his heart.

"Nice one," she said, and just to show Mike there were plenty of hard feelings, she leaned over and kissed her driver on the cheek.

"Oh, man, I feel lucky already," he said.

Taylor had forgotten how good barbecue could be. Most of the athletes drank water or soda, Dylan ordered a bottle of his sponsor's beer, and Kendall had a margarita. Taylor joined Dylan in a beer, and noticed that Mike did the same.

Taylor mostly listened. She found the conversation fascinating. This was insider stuff. The talk turned to Daytona last year, where Dylan had made a poor showing. "He had some trouble in Turn Two," Hank said, and they all laughed. It was one of those NASCAR lines her dad loved to spout. He used it for all sorts of occasions, when the washing machine broke, or he was home late, he'd bellow in his fake southern radio announcer voice, "Had some trouble in Turn Two."

She wished, not for the first time today, that her dad were here. He would have loved this so much. Without knowing she did it, she turned her gaze to Mike and found him looking her way, and she knew he'd read her mind. The second he heard that phrase he'd thought of her father, also. Her breath hitched for a second and then she forced her gaze away, across the table to where Jeff was telling a mildly amusing story about a recent pit crew drill.

When everybody had finished eating, Hank said, "Listen, Dy, I've got to be up early tomorrow. I'm trying out a new vehicle on the local track."

"Right. We should get going."

There was general agreement and everybody rose. She shot a quick look at Mike and found he hadn't moved. He was leaning back in his chair, half a beer left in his glass, and he was staring at her. His message was as clear as if he'd spoken. "We need to talk."

She nodded once, and said, "Dylan, if you don't mind, I might use this opportunity to do some sucking up to that columnist you wanted me to impress. I'll catch a cab back to my car."

Dylan sent her a glance of approval and slipped his arm across Kendall's shoulders. "Sure, okay."

"What time should I meet you out at the track, Hank?"

"You don't have to—"

"I'd like to spend all of tomorrow shadowing you if you don't mind. I think it will help me do my job."

"Okay. How's seven?"

She nodded. "I'll be there."

"You're sure you want to do this?"

"Hank, I am new at this. I need to get to know you a little bit."

He sent her a crafty look. "I'm planning to do some rock climbing."

What? Did he think she'd spent her life painting her nails? "Indoor or out?"

He cracked a grin. "In."

She nodded. "I'll need to rent gear, and I'm a little rusty, but I'm game."

"Excellent. See you at seven."

While everybody was saying their goodbyes, she took her time moving down to sit beside her ex-husband.

He flagged a passing waitress, pointed to his almost empty beer and held up two fingers.

Soon they were alone, at a long table with the remains of a messy dinner, sipping beer.

"Seems like old times," Mike said at last, turning away from the table slightly so he was facing her.

"Not really."

He sighed. "No." There was another awkward pause, then he said, "You chopped your hair off."

And didn't that summary of her looks make her feel like a million bucks. "It's chin-length, very fashionable in surfing circles." She shrugged. "I got used to a carefree lifestyle. Everything I owned fit into a backpack. Except my surfboard. No room for a blow-dryer." She pushed her fingers through her hair and let it fall. "Easy."

"It's good you're used to living out of a backpack. It'll be easier for you to spend half your life on the road with your driver."

She was certainly an expert at moving on.

"You look good," he said. "Australia suited you."

She watched the bubbles in her beer glass. "It's a great place. Hot."

"What did you do there?"

"Surf, mostly. Some scuba diving. Sightseeing."

"Work at all?"

She shrugged, uncomfortable telling him how little she'd done, she who used to be so ambitious, and wondering why she should care what he thought of her. "Some freelance travel articles."

"Nice life."

She ignored the slight edge of sarcasm. "It was. But now I'm home. I have a new job."

Home.

A vision of Mike carrying her across the threshold of the house they'd bought together in Seattle's Queen Anne Hill struck her like the big curl of a surf wave. *Bam*. They were both in grubby jeans with a car full of cleaning supplies and a few boxes of stuff to move in. He'd opened the door with the key they'd picked up at the Realtor's, and then, before she could take a step inside, had hauled her up in his arms. She was so surprised she dropped her mop and rubber gloves on the porch. They'd been laughing as they stepped through the front door.

She'd believed they'd live in the old character home together all their lives, fixing it up, raising a couple of kids.

The marriage hadn't lasted three years, and she hadn't stopped wandering since it ended.

He flicked a glance her way but didn't call her on the fact that home, for her, had never been in North Carolina.

His gaze rested steadily on her face. "Why are you here, Taylor?"

"Because I got offered a great job."

"There are jobs all over the country. Even in Australia, I bet."

"Of course there are, but…" As the meaning behind his words sank in she found herself growing wide-eyed with a combination of surprise and horror. "You don't think…? You can't imagine for one second that I took this job because you were here?"

"That unlikely but flattering possibility had crossed my mind."

"Well, wipe it right out of there." She leaned forward, dropping her voice so the waitress currently clearing the table wouldn't hear her. "Do you think for one second that I would deliberately put myself anywhere near you?"

He looked at her impassively. It was impossible to read what was going on in his eyes, eyes so dark they appeared almost black in the dim light of the restaurant.

When he didn't speak, she continued, "It's a coincidence. A sick joke of fate. A—"

"How'd you find out about the job? I doubt it was posted in the *Sydney Herald*."

"No. Of course not. Reena e-mailed me. She had an opening for a PR manager and she thought of me because—" She cut herself off as she saw Mike's brows rise. Reena was one of her parents' oldest friends. She'd been present at the party they'd held to celebrate their marriage, had visited her and Mike several times when she'd been in Seattle. "Because she knows me and that I love racing and have the skills required for the job."

"I see."

"Reena must have known you were here."

Mike nodded, in a "duh" way.

"But she never breathed a word to me." She drew in a couple of quick, shallow breaths. "She's a family friend! How could she not tell me that if I took the job, I'd have to work with you? I can't believe she would do anything so cruel to me."

"Don't be melodramatic. Reena's crazy about you."

"Then why would she…"

Once more her words petered out. Mike leaned back in his chair and folded his arms across his chest. "I would guess that your old family friend is trying her not-so-subtle hand at matchmaking."

"Matchmaking? What is she, crazy? We hate each other."

"Be careful with the word 'we.' I've got divorce papers that stipulate there is no 'we.'" He leaned forward, uncrossing his arms. "And you have no idea how I feel about you."

CHAPTER FOUR

SHE FOUND HER GAZE DROPPING to the table. "Why did you leave Seattle?"

"For a lot of the same reasons you did, I guess. I'm surprised nobody ever told you."

"None of my friends or family are allowed to mention your name." She glanced up defiantly. "It's a rule."

"I see."

She tapped her fingernails on the table. "What a mess."

"Oh, yeah. Quite a mess."

"How long have you been here?"

"About ten months. Eleven, maybe."

"So, you left right after…"

"Right after I sold the house, the car, packed everything up and said my goodbyes. I didn't have the same luxury you did of being able to up and leave everything."

"I—I guess I thought you'd stay."

They both watched the waitstaff carrying away empty plates and glasses, restoring order. Mike said, "What are you going to do?"

"Do about what?"

"Are you going to stay or head out again?"

She wanted to run so badly her feet were getting hot. But she shook her head. "I thought about telling them I made a mistake and getting the first plane out of here, but I can't. I made a commitment to Reena and to Hank. We agreed on a three-month trial."

"A three-month trial." He rolled the words around in his mouth as though they might have a flavor. "That's a good idea. No long-term obligation. If you and the job don't suit, no problem. Everybody moves on. It should be standard in employment contracts." He leaned closer and dropped his voice. "Wouldn't be a bad idea in marriage contracts."

A headache was beginning to throb behind her left eye. "Please don't bring up our marriage. This situation is enough of a nightmare."

To her great surprise, he started to laugh, a low chuckle. "You have to admit there is a certain irony to us both moving far away and taking new jobs, only to find ourselves working together again."

"It's certainly made for an unforgettable first day on the job."

"Started off my racing season with a bang."

She considered the ramifications of this new relationship. "Speaking of us working together, I hope you won't let our past relationship interfere in the way you treat Hank."

All vestige of amusement left his face in an instant. He leaned forward, his voice low and intense.

"First, I hate that word 'relationship.' We had a marriage. It may have been a lousy one, but give it the dignity of calling it what it was. Second, I've made a name for myself with this column. The reason so many people read it is because I'm fair. I play no favorites, I don't jerk anybody around."

"I'm not saying—"

"Hank's a good kid. He's starting out and he's got a lot of potential, but there's also a big downside for him. He's one of three rookie drivers this year. He's coming in with some good credentials and I'm watching him like everybody's watching him. He won't get more ink because we used to be married and he won't get less."

She knew he spoke the truth and felt ashamed of herself for even hinting otherwise. Mike might have been a crap husband but he was a good man and he'd always been a fair reporter. "I had to bring it up."

"Part of your job, as Dylan so eloquently put it, is sucking up to me. You might want to start working on that."

"Oh, and aren't you going to love that."

He didn't quite smile, but she knew him well enough to know the restraint cost him. "I'm human."

"So you say."

"Hey, Mikey!" a male voice bellowed, and Taylor turned at the same time Mike did to see a trio looking like they were out to party. The guy was probably in his early thirties and with him were two women about Taylor's age, young, hip and trendy.

"Jay, my man," Mike said, rising and shaking hands.

The guy called Jay looked at Taylor and Mike and at the long table. "Did you scare all your friends away?"

"Not me. Taylor here. She's Hank Mission's new PR manager. Taylor, this is Jay Barnham, a local reporter."

"Hi," he said, and they shook hands. "Tracy and Natasha are both in PR. They're in town for a convention and we hooked up." After a general greeting, Jay said, "Why don't you two come join us for a drink?"

"Sure," Mike said. "You go ahead. Taylor is doing a big suck-up job on me. I should let her finish."

Jay laughed. "Got it. See you in a minute."

"You're enjoying having me at your mercy way too much."

"Makes a nice change from our marriage."

Her jaw dropped. "That's not true. I—"

"Okay, forget I said it. This is weird for both of us. But here's what I want to know."

Her brows rose in a silent question.

"How do we handle this?"

She let out a breath. "I don't know. When we saw each other at the rookie thing, we played it like we'd never met before. I guess we should stick to the script."

"Fine by me." There was another pause. How were they ever going to work together if they couldn't even breathe the same air comfortably?

She'd made a three-month commitment to Hank, and she tried to honor her commitments. Okay, so the for-better-for-worse-till-death-do-us-part commitment hadn't worked out so well, but then she didn't think she was entirely to blame for her marriage hitting the dust with all the grace and subtlety of a tornado.

Around them the restaurant was busy with groups talking and laughing over a shared meal. The smell of barbecue warmed the air. And here they were, two people stranded among the mess of a dinner party that was over. It seemed somehow symbolic. For the next three months at least they were going to have to work together, and she thought they'd have a better chance if they tried to act polite. So she sucked in a breath and took on her first and probably toughest PR task.

"How have you been?" she asked at last.

"Fine. Good."

"You've put on weight," she said, then could have bitten her tongue. What was wrong with her? "But it's fine. It looks good on you." She'd always liked the little bit of roundness to him. And when he glanced at her out of the corner of his eye she knew he was thinking, as she was, how she'd always called him her teddy bear. Nauseatingly stupid pet name. She was the biggest idiot on the planet.

"You've lost some weight."

"Yeah." She'd left so much of her old life behind, from her blow-dryer—who needed it with a short, breezy cut—to the wedding dishes—who needed a set of twelve anything? She had exactly two plates, bowls, glasses, cups and cutlery. She'd rented a furnished apartment until she got settled and looked around.

Simple. Uncluttered. No ties.

"You could have sent a postcard."

"A postcard? What would I have said?"

He sent her a hard look. "That you were okay."

A prickle of guilt crossed her skin. She scrunched her toes inside her pumps, a nervous habit. "It never occurred to me you'd be worried."

He shook his head. "Doesn't matter. I needed to know you were okay, that's all. Call it closure."

"How'd you find out?"

"Don't worry, none of your family or friends gave you away. Not even Reena. I improperly used office resources at the paper and tracked you down."

"Oh. Sorry." She could have e-mailed him from an Internet café somewhere. It wouldn't have killed her. But the truth was she couldn't even think about him without it hurting too much to bear. Writing to him would have been awful. What if he'd written back?

There was another silence. She remembered in the old days how they couldn't seem to talk fast enough, they had so much to say to each other. Now she couldn't think of any subject that wouldn't lead to awkwardness.

"So, you want to join Jay and his friends?" She

could imagine Jay and Mike and the two women having plenty of fun without an ex-wife clogging up the picture. She tried not to imagine which of the two Mike would end up subtly paired with as the evening wore on. She didn't want to know.

She shook her head. "I'm still jet-lagged. I need to get to bed."

"Come on," Mike said. "I'll drive you back to your car."

She was surprised he'd offer, but then he'd always been the kind of man who'd change a light bulb you couldn't reach or who'd remember to pick up milk on his way home without being asked. "I'm getting a cab. And so should you. I saw you drink three beers." She only hoped the fact that he had downed three beers dulled his attention to the fact that she had noticed. She was acting like a wife.

But he didn't call her on it. "Right. We'll get a cab."

"I'll get my own cab." She stood and picked up her bag. "Are you coming?"

His gaze rested on hers for a moment. "No. If you don't need me, I'll go join Jay. See you later."

If you don't need me. Oh, Mike, she thought, *where were you when I really did need you?*

Would he hit it off with one of the PR women? They both looked like a lot of fun, and were clearly attractive. Or, for all she knew, he already had a girl-friend. It hadn't occurred to her that he'd be seeing somebody and the thought gave her an odd pang, but the chances were good. He was fun to be with, attractive in his way. Single.

He'd always been responsible, never drinking and driving, but she wasn't sure she even knew him anymore. "Do I need to steal your keys?"

"No. I'm not stupid." He glared at her. "And you are not my wife."

She turned and stalked toward the exit. "Lucky me."

MIKE WATCHED TAYLOR WALK away—something he'd sworn to himself he'd never do again—and once she was out of sight he wandered to the bar area of the restaurant, where he could see a screen in the corner flickering with a tennis match. Ironically, it turned out to be the Australian Open.

Australia! There ought to be some kind of prize for a man who not only drove his beloved wife away, he drove her to the other side of the planet.

He stared at the figures battling out Down Under. Didn't matter. Sports was sports, and something about the televised version soothed him and helped him think. What he needed was some clarity on this situation.

Jay and his friends were part of a big, laughing group at a table in the back. Mike did not feel like being part of a big, laughing group right now. He felt like being alone with a big sports screen.

However, the guy beside him had other ideas, and they quickly struck up one of those basically anonymous sports conversations. Soon he was drinking Scotch with his new buddy and putting his problems aside for a couple of hours. They'd find him again soon enough, he knew.

The whole Taylor thing was a disaster, but the more Scotch he downed the more fuzzy his problems seemed. He knew the booze-induced haze would be temporary, but if a guy wasn't allowed to get plastered after coming face-to-face with the woman he thought he'd finally got out of his system, only to find he'd been fooling himself, then he couldn't think of a better occasion.

Some time later, after Jay and his group had left, he was thinking he should find that cab and haul his butt home, when he felt a tap on his shoulder.

He turned. Squinted. Dylan Hargreave stood before him, in the same leather jacket he'd been wearing before and with his car keys in his hand and another jacket folded over his arm. "Dy? What you doing here?"

"Kendall forgot her jacket in the cloakroom. I saw your car still in the lot. You need a ride home, buddy?"

"Don't bother." He waved a hand in the air. "I'll call a cab."

"It's no trouble. Come on. Let's get you home."

There was a tap on his other shoulder. He turned and his tennis buddy said, "See that guy there?"

"Yeah."

"He's a NASCAR driver." In a loud whisper, he said, "I forget his name, but I think he's famous."

He patted his new friend on the back. "I know. See you."

He shook his head in Dy's direction. "Poor guy's had a few. Not himself." He swallowed the last of the liquid in his tumbler and said goodbye to the whole bar. Most of them knew him by now, so he got a cheerful farewell.

Dylan seemed amused by him. There was probably a reason. He'd think about it in the morning.

Luckily, Dylan knew where he lived. He and some of the other boys had played poker together at Mike's place, so Mike didn't have to concentrate on giving Dy directions, which was good. The road seemed windier than he remembered and the sky wouldn't stay in one place. When they arrived at his town house, he found his driver walking to the door with him. He was a bit unsteady on his feet, but he had his pride. "I'm okay. Fine."

"Where are your keys? I'll get you inside." Dylan shook his head. "I wouldn't want to have your head tomorrow."

Mike fumbled in his pocket and pulled out his keys, wishing they wouldn't make quite so much noise knocking together.

"Believe me, you wouldn't want my head tonight, either. I wish I could get the damn woman out of my mind." Dylan got the door open and Mike held on to the door frame as he entered his town house. "I tried, you know."

"Uh-huh."

The door shut behind them. Couple of stairs to navigate, but he could handle it. It was Taylor being in town that was going to be tough. "Of all the gin joints, in all the world, she had to walk into mine," Mike mumbled.

"Okay, up the stairs. Let's get you to bed."

"I'm fine."

"You're quoting *Casablanca*. Proving you are not fine."

"*Casablanca*." He snorted in derision. "A movie about losing the same woman twice. And you know what?" Mike turned, using his hands to help him make his point, and almost toppling before he righted himself. "Women love that movie. Can't get enough of it. You know why?"

"Keep moving. We're almost there."

They were in his bedroom. Oh, good. His bed. He really needed to lie down. He pulled off his jacket, dropped it on the chair in the corner, and it slid to the floor. "I'll tell you why. They're all the same, women. Kick a man until he's down and then kick him again." His head hit the pillow and came up again. "Harder."

Dylan's voice came from the doorway. "This woman who's got you all tied up, she got a name?"

He snorted. "Oh, yeah. She's got a name. And it's not mine. She wouldn't take my name, either. Should have known then. Thought she was a modern feminist, but that wasn't it." He shook his head and then stopped because the room was swimming. "She didn't take my name so she'd never have to give it back."

He heard water running and some clinking noises, and then Dy reappeared with a glass of water and a bottle of aspirin from the medicine cabinet. "I'm guessing you'll need these."

"Thanks." He struggled to his elbow and downed some water, sluicing liquid down his chin. "You know, you're a good friend, Dy." He nodded sagely. "Good driver, too."

Mike got a snort of laughter in return. "I wish you were writing your column right now. I have a feeling I'd come out looking pretty good." He pulled off Mike's shoes and dropped them to the carpet. "If anyone could make sense of it."

"No. It's true. You're all right."

"So are you. Take it easy."

"I need some sleep, that's all."

A low chuckle answered him. "You sure do."

"Dylan?"

"Yeah?"

"A woman should stick. Don't you think?"

Dylan turned back. "I do. And the right woman will stick."

"Hah." He heard his own world-weariness in the single syllable. "That's what you think. You're in love. You poor schlep."

The bedroom light flicked off. Vaguely, he heard the front door to his town house close.

His last thought was, why?

Why did she have to come back?

MIKE WOKE TO THE NEW DAY with a pounding head and a vague feeling that he might have had one Scotch too many. Rising slowly, he downed the glass of water he found at his bedside and shook out a couple of aspirin, pleased that he'd thought ahead. He must be getting smarter as he got older.

He padded to the kitchen still in the clothes he was wearing from last night, started a pot of coffee and, while it brewed, stripped and stuffed himself into a long, hot shower.

By the time he'd shaved, drunk two cups of coffee, eaten some toast and dressed, he was functional. Maybe he wouldn't be trail-riding or tap-dancing in the next few hours, but he was on his feet and moving.

For one long, dazed moment outside by his parking spot, he thought his car had been stolen. Then he remembered that it was still at the restaurant. And that Dylan had driven him home in his less-than-sober state.

He didn't like appearing like that in front of a driver. But if it had to be anybody, he was glad it was Dylan. Dylan was a good guy. One of the best, and as much as a columnist reporting on racing could be friends with one of his subjects, they were friends.

He'd said some stuff last night, he was sure he had. Only he couldn't remember what.

Probably he should warn Taylor that he might have slipped up. But he didn't want Taylor to know he'd drunk himself silly last night because she'd come back. Or that he'd been so glad to see her again—setting eyes on her last night had been like the very first time he saw her when every fiber of his being had shouted, *Yes!*

Had he learned nothing?

How could he be so stupid?

How could he still want the woman who'd stomped all over his heart?

CHAPTER FIVE

TAYLOR DROVE INTO THE Winfield Racing lot in the funky little Toyota Echo she'd leased the day before, right after returning from her very satisfactory climbing expedition with Hank.

The physical exertion had helped get rid of some of the tension flooding her body since discovering Mike worked in the same industry in the same town. But, once her irritation dimmed, she found that she and her driver were both having fun climbing. He was focused, tenacious and determined to succeed, qualities she had expected to find in him.

That she had the very same qualities had obviously come as a bit of a surprise to Hank. Especially when she outscored him. She was still smiling when she recalled the expression on his face. He'd been a good sport, though, and she had a feeling that with a few hours of climbing, they'd bypassed weeks of getting to know each other.

As she pulled into an empty parking space, she had no doubt the car would get her laughed out of the employee parking lot by the guys in their big trucks.

She didn't care. She intended to set herself apart from the gearheads and drivers. She was in the image business now, and she might as well start with her own.

She and Hank were both starting from scratch, she reasoned as she parked her little red car between a black Dodge Ram and a gleaming silver Yukon. When she got out and turned back to lock the doors, her tiny car looked like their offspring.

Day three of her new job in North Carolina. Here, she'd make a new start. Here, she was ready to settle. She'd felt so confident of her future that, on impulse, she'd bought herself a house plant—okay, so it was a ficus, which was only slightly less indestructible than a plastic plant. But for her it was a symbol. She was putting down roots again. And this time, she wouldn't make stupid mistakes—like marrying a man such as Mike Lundquist. This time, she'd get it right.

She crossed her eyes to check out how her moisturizer was holding up and saw the telltale white. Her nose was peeling again.

When she entered the building, she took one step toward her own office, then turned to track down the woman who hired her.

Never put off until tomorrow what you can do today, her mom used to say. She'd died when Taylor was sixteen. Dropped dead of an aneurism while she was cooking dinner. There were times, lots of times in the past few years, when she longed to be able to pick up the phone and hear her mother's voice. At odd times, like now, she'd hear her, though, as clearly as though she were in the room. She wondered what her mother would think of her old friend's behavior and was pretty certain she would not approve.

Reena was great. She'd tried to be there as a surrogate mom for Taylor, but she'd never be the same kind of woman—as witnessed by this appalling stunt she'd pulled, luring Taylor to Charlotte and conveniently forgetting to tell her that Mike was here.

She found Reena in her office surrounded by paperwork. Family photos lined the credenza behind her and potted plants dotted the room, each one thriving. The woman even had an orchid in bloom. Taylor got the feeling she'd never embrace the notion of clutter-free. Among the parade of figurines on the windowsill was a praying angel that had to be a Christmas ornament and a green porcelain money bank in the shape of a hat and decorated with shamrocks that screamed Saint Patrick's Day.

She'd prettied up a black leather couch with a scatter of stuffed animals, the way another decorator might use throw pillows. A feather boa and castanets hung together from one wall that Taylor didn't even want to ask about.

"Good morning, Reena."

"Morning, Taylor. How's it going?" Reena glanced up from an open file folder and slipped off her reading glasses. She was obviously busy, as the gesture seemed to imply, but would make time for her new PR manager.

In spite of the informality of her office, Reena wasn't a woman who wasted time at work, so Taylor got right to the point.

"I met an old friend the other night."

Reena didn't quite blush, but she did drop her gaze to the open file. She didn't waste time, either. "Mike. I figured you two would bump into each other before long."

She wouldn't get mad, Taylor reminded herself, as she had about fifty times since she'd bumped into Mike. "I wish you'd told me he was here."

"Nobody was allowed to mention his name. Your rule."

"But—"

"Okay. I deliberately didn't tell you he was here because I figured you wouldn't take the job if you knew. And frankly, that would have been a mistake. This is a great opportunity for you. And it was time to come home to the States. You couldn't spend all your life wandering." Her forehead was creased in concern. "Now that both your parents are gone, I guess I thought I should do what they would have wanted. I should bring you home. When this job came up I knew it was meant to be."

Sometimes well-meaning friends were the worst. "I'm not sure it's going to work, me and Mike in the same city."

"Well, hon, you've only signed on for a three-month trial. If it doesn't work—" she flapped the papers around as she threw up her hands "—it doesn't work. And you can get on with the rest of your life. But I would hate to think that Mike Lundquist would stop you taking a great job."

Taylor sank to the couch and fiddled with the ears of Minnie Mouse. "Mike suggested you were trying your hand at matchmaking," she said.

"Why would I do that? You two are divorced."

"Exactly." She nodded. The reporter in her noted that Reena hadn't denied Mike's accusation. She'd answered with a question. "And we're going to stay that way."

"Fine by me."

"All right, then."

"Was there anything else?"

"Hank got a new sponsor," she said.

Reena's mouth relaxed into a smile. "I heard. The plumbing-supply chain. That's great."

Taylor dropped Minnie and picked up a stuffed bear of the sort won in carnival shooting galleries. "Weren't you worried that in hiring me you weren't doing Hank any favors?" She smoothed the bear's paws where tufts of fur stuck up. "I mean, what if Mike won't cover Hank or whatever because he's avoiding me?"

"I think too highly of both of you to consider for one moment that your past personal history would get in the way of your professionalism," she said, with a slight edge that Taylor supposed was meant to be a warning.

"Of course, but we're not exactly friends."

Reena walked out from behind her desk and came to sit beside Taylor. "He called me, after you'd left for Australia. Taylor, he was frantic. I didn't tell him where you were, of course, because you made us all swear we wouldn't tell him a thing, but it was tough not to crack. He was seriously worried about you."

Bitterness welled within her. "Maybe if he'd been more worried about me when we were married, things would have turned out differently."

"It was a difficult time," she said gently. "For both of you."

"I'm pretty independent, but when I lost Dad and then...the baby, I didn't know what to do. I needed him."

"I know." Reena's voice was as soothing as a hug.

"And the more I needed him the more he kept disappearing to work or to watch TV. It's like he was only in love with me when life was easy. The minute things got tough he bolted." She sat the bear back down beside her. "I can't be married to a man like that."

"Did you ever talk to him about how you felt?"

"Talk to him? I could barely find the man."

"Counseling?"

"Please. To Mike the miscarriage was no more than a hiccup."

Reena nodded. "Men don't think of a pregnancy as a real baby until it's born. But we do."

"The second I found out I was pregnant I was planning the kid's life." Even talking about this with

Reena was tough. The hollow feeling she'd carried around so long came back. Empty-womb syndrome, she called it.

She had loved that baby with all her heart, talked to it when no one was around, slipped into children's specialty stores and pored over the tiny sleepers and dresses and overalls. "I still have dreams where I hear a baby crying and I'm trying to get to it but I can't find it." She stopped, swallowing hard.

"I'm sorry, honey," Reena said, rubbing her back.

She shook her head helplessly. "It's just one of those things. I'll get over it."

"Sounds to me like you and Mike might still have some unfinished business."

"Oh, no," she said, jumping to her feet. "No, we don't. We're divorced. That's finished business."

"Okay," Reena said mildly.

She turned to the door.

"Did you meet any nice guys in Australia?"

"Sure. Lots." Though in truth most had seemed either too young or too unfocused to appeal to her.

"Did you have any relationships?"

"Reena, I'm barely divorced."

The woman drilled her with her eyes. "Did you have a single date?"

"I don't have time for this. I need to check that the plumbing-supply logo's being put on Hank's car correctly."

CHAPTER SIX

"HEY, TAYLOR!"

She glanced up from the schedule she was working on. Daytona was a week away and the air at Winfield was thick with hope, excitement—the busywork of preparation. She was as fired-up as anyone.

"Hank, how are you holding up?" She couldn't imagine what he must be feeling. The pressure on him to do well at Daytona was a heavy burden. He seemed his usual self, but more fidgety than normal. She wanted to help him, but she was sure a pep talk from her would be frowned on by all. He had a sports coach, for goodness' sake, hired by Gordon Winfield himself, the billionaire owner of a string of home-improvement stores as well as Winfield Racing, and a man who believed in performance coaching in every level of his organization, from his stock clerks to his stock car drivers.

"Great," he said, his body half in and half out of her office. He often talked to her from the doorway, as though he couldn't stand to have his whole body inside an office. She got the feeling he was happiest outside. And if he had to be inside, he'd stay as close to a door as possible.

"Need a favor."

"Sure."

"I had an idea." He bounced on the balls of his feet as though getting ready to throw hoops.

She rose and walked around her desk so she could see him better. When she did, she thought he looked mildly embarrassed. "Yes?"

"When Dy was racing, before Kendall came along, he always had somebody really hot at the race with him. Like a date."

"Sure. I remember." Dylan had been known for the gorgeous women he brought to races—a new one every week. She recalled how much more interest she'd taken in Dylan Hargreave's career when Kendall Clarke arrived on the scene and their pre-race kisses had become something of a racing legend. Never had she seen any driver's stats go up so fast and so consistently as Dylan's had done once he started kissing Kendall.

The quiet actuary, so different from Dy's usual companions, had quickly become known as his good-luck charm. Of course, now she'd seen them together and knew the story better, she suspected that Dylan had found the right woman to spend his life with. That was the good-luck charm.

"Well, I was thinking I should do that."

"I'm not quite with you. Do what?"

He was doing isometric bicep exercises on her door frame. "Take hot women to races."

"Oh. Okay. I don't see why not."

"Good." He stopped exercising long enough to pull a scrap of paper out of his pocket. "So, can you set it up?"

He handed her a crumpled paper that had started life as a napkin. When she smoothed it out, she read *Denise* scrawled in pen and a phone number. She looked up at him. "You want me to ask this woman on a date?"

"No. Well, sort of. I met her at a photo shoot." She had a feeling this was one part of her job that had the possibility to become complicated.

"Oh, she's a photographer."

"Very funny. She's a model."

"No!" The woman had drawn a loopy heart over the *I* in Denise.

"Can you organize her time when she's at the track? Make sure she's taken care of?"

"Sure."

"Thanks." He started cracking his knuckles.

"Hank?"

"Uh-huh?"

"I've got my sports bag in the car. Do you want to go for a run or something?"

He looked at her as though she were a brain surgeon who'd successfully removed a life-threatening tumor. "Oh, yeah, that'd be great. I've got some energy to burn off. Can you tell?"

There were sweat marks on her door frame and he'd nearly worn shoe treads into her carpet with his restless feet. "A lucky guess. Come on."

They ran for more than an hour. The countryside here was still new to her. Most of the racing teams were headquartered out of town, not too far from the Charlotte track, so they were able to run on relatively flat roads, by green fields dotted with trees she couldn't yet name. That was the fun of moving to a different place, she thought, everything was new.

The weather was warm but not hot, and she and Hank found a nice rhythm. They didn't talk much, she figured they both needed the stress release more than they needed chitchat.

It was an odd way for her to spend an hour in the middle of a busy day, but she'd already learned that keeping Hank happy was her number-one duty, and, besides, she liked the man.

His legs were longer and he had a loping stride, but after a year of surfing, swimming, tennis—what seemed now, looking back, like a year of summer camp—she was as fit as she'd ever been and had no trouble lengthening her stride and keeping up.

They returned to the Winfield building sweat-soaked and, at least in Hank's case, a little calmer. Probably she was better for the workout, too, she thought, as they cruised into the parking lot at a slow, cool-down jog. She was carrying a load of stress, too, as her first race approached. Would she forget something vital? Screw up Hank's schedule? Mess up with the media?

She was determined she wouldn't, but it didn't stop her from waking up in the middle of the night panicked. She kept a notebook and pen by her bed and took to scrawling herself reminder notes, half of which she couldn't read come morning.

She'd spent a lot of time getting to know Hank's crew chief, the guys in the pit crew, most of whom worked at Winfield racing full-time. She timed pit drills for them, got to know the routines and the lingo. It would be her job to watch every race from the pit, finding tidbits she could feed to the media during races, and then preparing a post-race report. She was the person who would feed Hank's information out to the world. It was an onerous responsibility, but she was determined to do well.

It was also her job to make sure all the sponsor decals were on his car, and in the right spot. She bet she knew the paint scheme of his vehicle better than the painters did.

"Thanks, Taylor," Hank said. "That was great."

"It was good for me, too," she admitted, sucking back water. "I'm pretty tense."

He put his hands on her shoulders and rubbed them. "Ouch, hard as rock."

She dropped her head toward her chest in relief as his strong fingers kneaded the muscles. "I carry all my tension in my shoulders. Oh, that feels fantastic." She nearly moaned in relief, so lost in the sensation that she didn't hear the car pull in. She saw it, though, as it drove past and parked—and she felt her shoulder muscles retighten instantly as though somebody had yanked on a knot. Mike Lundquist's car.

Sure enough, he emerged from the driver's side. He wore dark sunglasses but she could tell he was observing her and Hank.

She could only imagine how it must look from Mike's point of view.

"Thanks, Hank. That was great," she said.

He removed his hands from her shoulders. "Sure. Anytime. Hey, Mike," Hank said when the columnist drew closer.

He received a nod. "Ready for the big day?"

Mike might have once been her husband, but right now he was part of the media, and in her role she needed to be clear that nobody interviewed Hank without setting it up with her first.

She let Hank say, "Sure," then in her politest tone, she said, "I don't have anything scheduled with you and Hank for today."

Hank headed inside with a final wave.

She felt Mike's gaze taking in her shorts and the running shirt that was plastered to her body with perspiration. His slow scrutiny from behind dark lenses infuriated her.

"No, you don't," he said in an equally pleasant and rather dismissive way.

He headed toward the front entrance.

She grit her teeth as he walked away from her.

She wouldn't run after him, so she raised her voice. "I need advance notice if you want to interview my driver."

Mike slipped off his glasses before entering the building. He turned to her. "I'm not here to interview your driver. I'm here to talk to Dylan." He opened the door, nodded politely and walked through it.

She stalked after him, hot, sticky and irritable. She grabbed the door before it had completely closed. Mike was chatting to the front-office receptionist, who told him that Jeff and Dylan would be out in a minute.

"Why don't you wait in my office?" Taylor said, sounding as businesslike as a woman in skimpy shorts sweating like a pig could sound.

She thought she saw Mike's mouth kick up, but he nodded and followed her. She led him down a gray-carpeted corridor with doors on either side. They could be in any office complex anywhere. Except that the view outside included bright-colored haulers emblazoned with Hank's and Dylan's pictures and those of their cars.

She walked into her office and he followed her, glancing around. "Nice," he said. "Basic, but nice." The office was sparsely decorated, with a desk, a computer and phone, a racing calendar on the wall and a framed photo of Hank beside his car. The walls were beige and the same gray carpet as the one in the hall covered her floor.

"After working in the bull pen of a daily newspaper, I am happy to have my own space." She glanced up at him where he stood looking around.

"No personal pictures? No memorabilia?" he asked, walking over to check out the single plant in her office, which she hadn't put there. It was healthy, so she was betting Reena had donated the fern.

"No. I keep my personal and work lives separate."

He sent her a quizzical glance but didn't remind her that she hadn't always done so.

When he'd finished his perusal of her work space she turned to him, crossing her arms across her chest.

"Why not?"

Mike looked questioningly at her. "Why not what?"

She pushed a lock of damp hair off her forehead irritably. "Why not interview Hank? He's the story at Winfield, the new man on the team. You should be talking to him."

"Honey, you're not the reporter here. You're the PR flack. I get to decide what the story is."

PR flack? That's how he saw her? They used to look down on journalists who did that, who traded the newspaper world for the corporate one of public relations and communications. Usually the money was a lot better, which only added to the notion of selling out.

She was about to launch into all the reasons why she was not a PR flack when she realized he was toying with her. As evidenced by the fact that he'd called her "honey," something he never even did when they were together.

Instead of rising to the obvious bait, she said, "Hank Mission is about to take Daytona and the NASCAR world by storm. He's fast, he's talented, he's fresh."

"That's why I want to interview him *after* Daytona. I'm interested in how he feels after his first race, not before."

"Oh."

"Is that okay? Can I have access?"

She raised her chin. "I'll have to see whether I can fit it into his schedule."

His eyes gleamed. "I'll call you to set something up."

A drop of sweat rolled down her temple. "Fine." Her office suddenly felt too small with Mike in it. She wished she hadn't so impulsively dragged him in here. She felt the heat coming off her body as she cooled down, and knew he was remembering, as she was, the times she'd dragged him off on a run. He always complained bitterly, but he wasn't a bad athlete when he bothered to get out there.

She wondered if he was getting any exercise at all without her to nag him. Then reminded herself that it wasn't her problem. She'd like to think that the legacy she'd left behind was one of a healthier diet and better exercise. However, she had a sneaking suspicion he'd backslid to his old unhealthy ways.

"Are you looking forward to Daytona?" he asked her.

"Yes. No. I'm so stressed I can't see straight. Which is why I'm off running when I have a million things to do. I think I want it to be over."

"It's a big deal, Hank's first race. How's he holding up?"

She narrowed her eyes. "Are you asking as a friend or as a reporter?"

"Neither."

Right, because they obviously weren't friends. And he wasn't here to do a story on Hank. She wondered how he would characterize their relationship if she asked, then she took one look at him and decided not to ask. "He's holding up really well. Better than I am."

"You're both going to be fine."

She nodded, grateful for even that much praise.

"Want some advice?"

"Sure."

"Relax. Pace yourself. At Daytona, spend some time in the media center getting to know everybody. This sport is all about relationships. You'll soon get a feel of what kinds of stories get picked up."

"Okay," she said, taking a deep breath. She'd always tried to do too much, too fast. No one knew that better than Mike. "Thanks."

"And get to know the pit reporters. They are the ones running around looking for interesting items throughout the race. You feed them information that the home viewer might want to know. Why you pitted suddenly, or what the driver said to his crew chief about the car and what they decide to do about it."

She nodded.

"You and the pit reporters can make one another look really good."

"Pit reporters. Right."

His lips twitched. "You're taking mental notes. Why do I think that the second I leave here you will be on that computer typing up what I just said?"

Because he knew her too well. He must know she was feeling a little overwhelmed. Anxious to do a good job, anxious for Hank. Tense that if she screwed up Mike Lundquist would be there to see it. "Okay, so I'm feeling like I'm scrambling to keep up. I'll get there."

"I know you will. Now, can I go see Dylan?"

"Of course."

"Thank you." He turned back. "And Taylor?"

"Yes?"

"One more piece of advice."

"What is it?"

His gaze traveled from her damp hair to her hot sneakered feet. "Take a shower."

CHAPTER SEVEN

DAYTONA BEACH, FLORIDA. Speedweeks. Taylor had seen glimpses of the beach every year on TV when she watched the race, but she'd never been here before. She took a deep breath of sea air and gazed out at the endless ocean while she cooled down after her run.

Hers were not the only feet jogging the beach. The sand was so hard-packed it was like running on a decent track. In the early days the stock cars had actually raced right here on the beach—she could almost imagine it, especially since cars were still allowed to drive onto the upper part of the beach.

Speedweeks was wild as fans piled in from all over, coming by plane, helicopter, boat and every possible motorized vehicle from motorcycles to pickup trucks. Then there were the RVs. Some cost more than most houses and others looked to be held together by rust and determination.

From the corporate CEO who came in his private plane to the everyday Joe who arrived in his beat-up pickup, you never knew who you'd rub shoulders with at the track.

Racing was everywhere; hotel lobbies sported bunting, fans went everywhere in racing gear and the corner stores couldn't keep the racing magazines in stock. Every television in every bar or restaurant in the city seemed to be tuned to the racing channel.

She had a precious few hours of downtime, and she used it to get out on the beach in front of the hotel where she and most of the other racing staff were staying. One of her more decadent lifetime goals was to walk, or even better, surf, every famous beach in the world. The weather in Florida, she'd been told, was uncertain this time of year, but today was magazine-cover perfect. The ocean was blue with just enough whitecaps to keep things interesting, the sand was hard packed and caramel-colored, and ahead of her stretched a line of hotels like a pastel Lego village.

Seagulls packed the beach and seemed to have picked up race-week fever, running in crazy circles when she approached. She took off her shoes and let her bare feet once again enjoy the feeling of rough sand beneath them. Tipping her head back, she let the sun warm her skin and then walked forward until her toes were in the water. It was cool but soothing, and to her mind, wading through ocean waves was a lot more therapeutic than a pedicure. Her feet were never happier than when shoeless and on a beach. Come to think of it, neither was she.

Deciding she could afford a few more minutes before dashing in for a quick shower and heading back out to the track, she sloshed her way through the cool water, thinking.

She loved her new job, but, of course, fate could never simply dish out the wonderful. Life's casserole always had something nasty, like turnips, to go along with the good stuff.

Mike was the turnip in her current casserole. And some days it felt like all she could taste was turnip. What was she going to do about him?

She looked off ahead to where couples strolled, joggers jogged and kids played.

Weird she should be thinking about Mike and then see a guy, one half of a chatting couple, who looked a lot like him. A few more steps with the cool water bubbling over her toes, and she still hadn't taken her eyes off the couple walking toward her. The guy started talking and gestured wildly with his hands. Even from here she could hear the young woman laugh.

It *was* Mike.

And he was with a woman.

A strange feeling kicked at her abdomen. She watched them, transfixed, as the space between them narrowed. She wondered if he'd even notice her as they passed, since he was so taken with his partner.

Then Mike looked ahead, right at her, and she saw his hands drop. Instead of veering away or pretending he hadn't spotted her, he deliberately changed their course so he and the woman were headed directly for her.

When they were close enough to converse, he said, "Taylor. Great timing."

It was? For whom?

"This is Louise Hunnicut." He waited. Like she was supposed to know who that was. She glanced politely at a lean young woman with dark red hair tied back, large hazel eyes, freckles, an uncompromising mouth and well-defined arm muscles.

"Hi," she said, "I'm Taylor Robinson."

"Tay, do you seriously not know who this is?"

Your new girlfriend? She shrugged. "Sorry."

"She won gold in the U.S. Road Racing Championships last year."

"Oh, congratulations. I was in Australia last year. I must have missed it."

"She's taking a training break right now. She's a NASCAR fan."

"Well, you're in the right place."

"I told her I have connections and could pull some strings."

Could he seriously be flirting with this much-younger woman, not to mention walking the beach with her at ten in the morning and not seem even a bit embarrassed to encounter his ex-wife? He was looking at her as if she was supposed to say something, when what she really wanted to do was whack him upside the head with her sweaty running shoes. "Good luck."

"She wants to meet Hank."

The breeze lifted strands of the woman's long red hair so the sun caught them. "Well—"

"I'm from Greenwood, South Carolina," the woman said, in an accent very much like Hank's. "'Bout an hour from where Hank grew up. I want to wish him luck, is all."

"Oh, I see." She had no idea, but she had a feeling Hank would want to meet another athlete who'd grown up near him. Seemed a Hank thing to do. "I'll have to check with him first. Is there somewhere I can reach you?"

"Um, I lost my cell phone, but—"

"If you call me, I can set it up," Mr. Helpful piped up.

Taylor nodded curtly. "Okay. I'll get back to you today. Enjoy Daytona," she said, and then continued on her way, walking an extra five minutes to be certain of not running into the pair again.

When her cell phone rang on her way back to the hotel, she wasn't surprised to hear Mike's voice. She felt as though she'd conjured him.

"There's a weird noise in the background," he said. "Are you still on the beach?"

"Yep."

He chuckled. "I should have known. Hank would get better help if he was a surfer."

Since she was pretty sure Mike was kidding, she let that one slide. "What do you want now? Track-side seats?"

"Hey, I bet I did you a favor. Hank will love meeting Louise."

She rolled her eyes. "I'm not promising anything except that I'll ask him."

"I didn't call about that. You know the interview I want with Hank?"

"Yes. I don't have his schedule in front of me, but I know you've got some time with him after the race."

"I've got a different idea."

"You have to interview him," she cried out. "You promised."

"Relax. I'm going to interview him. I'm thinking of doing a bigger profile. I want to include you."

"Me?" The word came out like a burp of horror. She was always the one behind the scenes, reporting on whoever was on center stage, never the one standing in the spotlight. Even now her job was behind the scenes. Hank was the one she wanted getting all the media coverage, not her.

Mike must know how she felt. He was doing this deliberately to annoy her. As though he hadn't annoyed her enough this morning. She was such an idiot. Of course he didn't want to interview her. "Why?"

"You're both new to racing. Hank's the new face on the track, but you are, too. I like the idea of talking to both of you. And you know what they say, behind every great NASCAR driver is a woman."

"No, I hadn't heard that one."

"Now you have."

"You're not serious." Beside her, a seagull pecked away at a jellyfish, exposed and helplessly out of its element. Which was pretty much how she felt right now.

"Of course I'm serious. Think about it from your end. Seventy-five million NASCAR fans and forty percent of them are women. I think female fans would be interested in your role in Hank's career."

"I think they'd be a lot more interested in Hank."

"I ran the idea past Gordon. He loves it."

She stubbed her toe against the hard sand, almost sending herself sprawling. "Gordon? You don't mean Gordon Winfield?" Her ultimate boss, the owner of Winfield Racing.

"He offered me a ride back in your company jet so I can interview you two together right after the race when it's all fresh."

"I don't know, Mike. Let me think about it."

"Sure. I'll be there on the plane, anyway."

Oh, great. Just great. She was sure he was doing this to her deliberately, to rattle her and probably to encourage her to quit her job and get out of his life and city one more time.

Which was blatantly unfair of him.

She ended the call, snapping her cell phone shut as though it were shark jaws.

SHE MADE HER WAY BACK to her suite and showered. She got out of the shower to the sound of her cell phone ringing and grabbed it in time to hear the good news. One more decal to add to Hank's car for the race. She'd learned that new deals were often inked during Daytona, which meant she had to stay on top of the sponsor decals. Today they'd be adding a soft drink manufacturer's logo to the B post on Hank's car. It meant more money for Hank's team, and more sponsorship appearances for her driver, as well as one more sponsor hat she'd have to remember to have him photographed in.

After she'd made certain that the decal was on the car and in the correct position, she made her way to Hank's motor home. No surprise, she heard the sounds of a video-game race in full swing coming from inside.

She entered to find Hank was not alone. He was racing his friend and mentor Carl Edwards. The two were utterly engrossed in the game until they saw her, then they both rose and greeted her with the good manners she'd come to love in well-brought-up southern men.

"Sorry, Hank. I didn't realize you had company. I can come back."

"It's okay. I paused the game. We're celebrating my new sponsor. You want one?" Hank pulled out a third can of soda from his new sponsor and she laughed as she accepted it.

On the table of his motor home, along with a computer and a pair of hand weights, was an eight-by-ten publicity picture of a stunning young woman with long, dark hair and big blue eyes. She wore a bikini that showed off a body that filled Taylor with momentary envy. The model looked like Angelina

Jolie without the tattoos. Seeing the direction of her gaze, Hank said, "That's Denise. The one I told you about. My date for the weekend races."

Carl moved closer and had a look for himself. He glanced up, nodding approval. "Nice-looking woman."

Hank blushed a little, she was certain, and tried to look nonchalant. "I met her at a photo shoot. She's a lot of fun."

"What's this under her arm?" Carl asked.

In truth, Taylor had been so struck by the way that woman filled out a bikini she hadn't noticed anything else, but on closer inspection, a small animal's head peeked out from the crook of Denise's arm.

They all craned over the table and Taylor read the printed script at the bottom of the photo. "Denise Lamott and her teacup Chihuahua, Cutie Pie, who goes everywhere with her."

"A teacup Chihuahua? What's that?" Hank asked, aghast.

"I don't know. But whatever it is it's pretty small. And kind of scrawny," Carl said.

"It's a dog," Taylor said. "Paris Hilton has one. Very trendy right now." Apparently, Denise Lamott had one, too. And it went everywhere with her. Great.

"My daddy's shot rats on the farm that were bigger than that. Better-looking, too." Hank looked closer. "Come to think of it, that there kind of looks like a rat."

"Except that Cutie Pie's wearing a sweater," his buddy kindly pointed out.

"She better not bring that thing with her. What am I going to do with a rat dog hanging around?"

"Says here, that dog goes everywhere with her."

Hank groaned and fell back into his chair. "That dog will ruin my reputation, my first race." He was so worked up his accent grew thick. Dog came out *daawwwg*. "What we need is a strategy."

She put her hand over the part of the photo that featured Cutie Pie, as though to protect him. "Hank Mission, don't you even think of doing anything to that dog."

Her driver looked at her as though she were a sick, sick woman. "I'd never hurt a dog," he said, looking as though he were the hurt one. "I meant a strategy for future race dates. This racing thing has more pitfalls than I knew." He shot a look at Carl. "You got any advice?"

"Besides a no-pets policy?" Carl sipped his drink and sat down again, his blue eyes thoughtful. "A weekend can be a long time to spend with someone you have nothing in common with." He didn't mention that Hank was likely to have nothing in common with Denise, but it was pretty obvious that's what they were all thinking. "You should figure out what you really want from these gals."

"I want somebody who looks good in front of the camera."

"Absolutely." Taylor thought about how many times Carl had shown up at races with his mom and how good she looked on his arm. She guessed Hank had some growing up to do. And some things to learn about women. "But you also want someone you can have fun with."

Hank nodded. "Makes sense."

"Knowing you, you want somebody with a sense of humor."

"Right."

Carl flicked a glance up at the paused video NASCAR game on the big screen. "If she likes video games, that would be a plus."

"Sure would."

"You like all sports," Taylor added. "It might help if she was athletic."

"Good one."

"And for me," Carl added, "I'm looking for a woman who likes dirt biking."

Hank looked impressed. "I could go for that."

He glanced at Taylor. "Can you remember all that?"

She got to her feet and headed for the door. "I'll never forget it," she said. "I'll draft a Ten Things Hank Mission Wants in a Woman list and post it to your fan site."

She turned to leave and said, "Oh, I forgot. There's a woman who wants to meet you. Come to think of it, she does like biking."

Both men glanced up at her with interest.

"She's a cyclist who grew up near Greenwood."

Hank laughed. "No way."

"Her name's Louise Hunnicut. She's some kind of—"

"Amateur women's Road Biking Champ?"

"Right. You know her?"

"No. Heard of her," Hank said. "I'd love to meet her."

"Okay. Mike Lundquist said he'd set it up."

Hank seemed immensely cheered and she figured so long as no one mentioned the words *teacup Chihuahua*, he'd stay that way for a while. "Why don't they both come over tonight? We're barbecuing at Dy's place. You come, too."

"That's okay, I don't need to come."

"I want you to. It'll be fun."

She nodded, thinking that when she'd decided to do whatever she could to make her driver happy, she hadn't counted on having to watch her ex make googly eyes at a cycling champion who was probably a decade younger than he was.

"You busy tonight?" Hank asked Carl.

"Yeah. Too bad. I'd like to meet her, too."

"Yeah. Too bad," Hank echoed, looking relieved.

WHEN TAYLOR ARRIVED FOR dinner that night, she found Mike and the cyclist were there ahead of her, as was Hank. The three of them were sitting in lawn chairs in front of Dylan's motor home. A portable barbecue was sending delicious scents into the air, and Kendall and Dylan were arguing about the amount of bourbon suitable for barbecue sauce. After greeting them and handing over the cake she'd brought, she left them to it.

Louise and Hank were already fast friends; in fact, they'd both lapsed into the thick South Carolina accent that Hank usually only spoke with when he was tired or excited.

Mike sat across from them in a lawn chair with a bemused expression on his face.

When he saw Taylor he nodded and pulled up another chair. She sat beside him.

"Do you have a single clue what those two are talking about?" he asked her.

"Nope."

"Amazing. So," he said, turning to her, "how are you doing?"

"Better than you."

"What do you mean?"

She nodded her head in the direction of the two young athletes. "If you don't do something soon, that rookie is going to scoop your date."

An odd look flashed across his face. He opened his mouth, then closed it. "Right."

CHAPTER EIGHT

IT WAS FRIDAY AFTERNOON and Denise was missing again. The model was more trouble than a bag of snakes. Hank had had her flown down yesterday in time for her to hang on his arm for the races Saturday and Sunday. It was pretty clear that apart from a shared interest in getting good photos for the media, the two of them had nothing in common.

Worse, as she'd feared, Cutie Pie, who was in her opinion very inappropriately named, had also arrived in his Louis Vuitton carry case.

Hank had competed in the NASCAR Busch Series race today, placing in the middle of the pack, which he'd seemed okay with. A number of drivers competed in both the NASCAR Busch and the NASCAR NEXTEL Cup Series. Some even drove in the truck race as well, so they ended up driving Friday, Saturday and Sunday. Not only did they stand to win decent prize money, but the extra races meant more time getting familiar with the track. Hank didn't race in the truck series, so she only needed to stay on top of two race schedules. It was a good thing she was naturally well organized, she thought as she made her way to his motor home.

As if Taylor didn't have enough to do on her first race week, she'd become the babysitter of a very pretty, very sweet and very dumb young woman who tended to wander.

Hank had also disappeared. Which he seemed to do every time he had to spend more than five minutes in Denise's—and Cutie Pie's—company.

Well, Denise wasn't Taylor's biggest priority. Hank was. His motor home was empty and his golf cart was missing.

And if she knew Hank, the first place he'd run to and hide at would be Dylan's.

She walked over to Dy's luxury coach, also parked on the infield in the special gated-off area. It was the millionaire's row of motor coaches, since they operated as homes away from home for drivers and their families. She suspected that some of the drivers spent more time in their coaches than they did in their own houses.

More than likely, Hank was racing Dylan on the latter's big-screen TV—one that was even bigger than Hank's.

She knocked on the door and heard Kendall say, "Come in."

Kendall Clarke was sitting with her feet up on the couch flicking through a magazine. There were no video-game noises, in fact, no noise of any kind. It was heaven.

"Hi," Taylor said, glancing around. "I'm looking for Hank."

"He and Dy went off somewhere in the golf cart. I wasn't really paying attention. I was reading." She gestured to the magazine on her lap.

"Well, if you see him will you tell him I'm looking for him? I'll let you get back to your magazine." She started to back out of the motor home.

"Don't go. I was just going to put on some coffee. You look as though you could use some."

The thought of spending time with a woman who wasn't going to talk nonstop racing was too tempting. There was something restful about Kendall. "You're sure?"

"Absolutely. I was reading a bridal magazine, but I don't know why I bother. They only depress me since I don't know when I'll ever be able to plan a wedding." She rose and started preparing coffee. Taylor was amused to see she started with fresh beans and ground them. She had a feeling Kendall loved everything done exactly right. "If only Dy's parents would go on a safari to Africa for a few months, somewhere where there was no communication with the outside world, I could plan the wedding, and when they got back from their trip there'd be nothing to do but show up." She sighed. "I dream of that safari."

Taylor set her cell to vibrate. "Any chance they'd take a trip like that?"

"Dylan's mother thinks leaving U.S. soil is unpatriotic."

"Challenging."

Kendall looked up and smiled. "Enough about me. How are you liking the new job?"

"Mostly I love it." She sighed and flopped down on the opposite couch. "Except for the babysitting requirement. I think Hank needs to refine his system of bringing gorgeous young things to the races with him."

Kendall laughed. "He needs to talk to Dylan. I believe the standard operating procedure is to fly them in for the race and then out again. Not spend three days with someone you barely know."

"Got it. I'll pass that on." She thought of Denise and her pint-size canine wandering goodness knew where. She'd have to track her down and make sure she didn't do or say anything that would reflect badly on Hank. "Believe me, I'll pass that on."

Those sharp eyes assessed her. "Or maybe he'll get smart and start hanging out with women he actually has something in common with. Like Louise, the biker from last night."

"I think Mike Lundquist might have something to say about that."

"Really?" Kendall scooped her freshly ground beans into a French press and poured boiling water over. The smell of coffee filled the air. "Seemed to me that Mike spent a lot of time talking to you."

She snorted. "Arguing, you mean. He's trying to

talk me into being part of a feature he's writing about Hank, which I really don't want to do."

Kendall nodded, then pushed the plunger down. "It sucks when your quiet, anonymous life gets taken away from you and you're pushed into the limelight. But it would be good publicity for Hank. How's he behaving, by the way? Apart from hiding from his date?"

"So far he's okay. I think he's watching me a little, judging me, but then I guess I'm doing the same thing."

"I heard you made a pretty good impression rock climbing. He said you beat him."

She laughed. "That was unusually honest in a man."

"I think he got a kick out of how good you are."

"One of the secrets of rock climbing is that a woman's body is actually better equipped to climb. Something to do with the center of gravity. But the fact that we both love sports definitely helped us bond."

Kendall nodded. "It's like with women, we'd go for lunch or go shopping to get to know each other. But for guys, all that stuff happens over sports. I think you two make a great team."

"Thanks." She kind of thought so, too, but it was nice to have confirmation. She and Hank had already reached an easy familiarity. She was finding she had to balance keeping his sponsors happy with keeping him happy. NASCAR was a huge media sport, and she knew it was important to find new ways to get him featured in the media since, as a rookie, he wasn't big news.

Yet.

She was starting to figure out which media were most important to his career. The most prestigious "gets" were the non-NASCAR media. That was where she was starting to put some effort, trying to find ways to connect Hank with mainstream media. She thought the rock climbing made a nice angle. He was also cute, young and single. She thought some of the women's magazines might find him quite appealing for a profile.

Thinking of Hank and women's magazines, she leaned forward and glanced over Kendall's shoulder, wondering if there was a bridal angle she could pursue. When her gaze landed on the magazine, all thoughts of Hank promptly deserted her. The full-picture spread was of a sumptuous wedding. There was a stack of all the newest bridal mags piled neatly on the floor at Kendall's feet. A shaft of pure feminine excitement shot through her.

"Oh, look how cute that little flower girl is."

The photo on the front of the magazine showed a girl of about three with big blue eyes and red ringlets of hair, wearing an embroidered green dress. A crown of flowers in her hair and a basket of rose petals completed the vision.

Kendall carried over a small tray with two sleek white mugs of perfect coffee, a matching cream-

and-sugar set and two shiny stainless-steel spoons. She'd added pale blue linen napkins to the tray.

"I know," she said, putting the tray down and reaching for another magazine. "And look at these three flower girls." She flipped open to where she'd put a sticky note on which she'd written a couple of lines in neat handwriting.

Sure enough, the picture was gorgeous. Girls in old-fashioned dresses with green sashes.

"Wait a minute. You bought every single bride magazine this month. And there are stickies in most of them. This looks to me like the cry for help from a desperate woman."

Kendall blushed and glanced all around before lowering her voice. "I am desperate. I love that man and I want to marry him properly. But what can I do when Dylan doesn't want to be swamped with media and fans, and we don't want his mother taking over everything?"

Not that Taylor was any expert, but Kendall's attitude did not bode well for mother-in-law-daughter-in-law relations. "It's tough to keep a family out of a wedding."

"His family will be invited, of course, but Dylan doesn't want his family knowing there's going to be a ceremony until the invitations go out and it's too late to turn the affair into one of his parents' gala events."

Taylor glanced at the photo spread out on Kendall's lap like a favored pet. "That layout you're drooling over isn't exactly no-frills."

"You don't understand. His parents will turn this into their event. I'm telling you, he still has nightmares about his first wedding. You know who sang 'Ave Maria'?"

She shook her head.

"Celine Dion."

"I love her voice."

"Me, too. But can you imagine? Dylan says there were two former presidents there—"

"NASCAR presidents?"

"I am referring to presidents of the United States."

"Oh, my."

"He lost count of the number of senators, big-shot business tycoons and minor royalty from Europe."

"That's some guest list."

"Dylan's family is very well connected."

"And you don't want that."

"It's complicated, but we need to do our wedding our own way. We need to live our lives our own way and that starts with our wedding."

"Sounds like a good idea."

"In theory it's great, but how do I put together a wedding in secret? Every wedding planner in the south has Dylan's mother on speed dial. Every caterer, wedding dress designer, stationer. That woman is the CIA, FBI and Omnimedia all rolled into one well-groomed package that scares the daylights out of me."

"How do you know? Maybe, since this is Dylan's second wedding, she won't care that much." Taylor added a splash of milk and stirred her coffee. When she tasted it the brew was, as she'd suspected, perfect.

"Hah. She told me she's got the entire wedding-planning community sewn up. Actually, she made it sound like a threat."

Taylor laughed. "She's got to be pulling your leg."

"That's what I thought. I immediately went to an out-of-the-way florist and asked a few questions about bridal flowers. Within twenty-four hours Dylan's mother was on the phone asking pointed questions. I won't even let Dylan buy me an engagement ring. I'm too freaked out by that family."

Taylor frowned, but then stated the obvious. "So, if you can't contact any wedding professionals, what are you going to do? Eloping is the obvious answer."

"I'm not going to elope. I plan to get married once. And I am going to do it right."

"Lucky you," Taylor said, trying not to appear sad, or cynical. She was the positive one, the optimist. The "let's put on a party" girl. She didn't rain on people's parades, especially not nice people like Dylan and Kendall, so she put on a happy face and said, "How are you going to sneak in a wedding with Dylan being a big news celebrity and his parents wanting to turn the event into a royal wedding?"

That sweet face toughened into stubborn lines. "I don't know. But I'll think of something. I want my wedding and I don't want it stolen from me."

"You couldn't go over to his home and tell his parents how you feel?"

"Which confirms my guess that you've never met Dylan's parents."

"No. I'll take your word for it they're a nightmare. Hmm." She thought for a minute. "You could do something completely untraditional, so you didn't need to visit the usual places."

Kendall wrinkled her nose. "Are we talking a muumuu wedding on Waikiki Beach?"

Taylor laughed at her new friend's expression. One more reason she was glad she wasn't married anymore. She no longer had to admit to her own Hawaiian beach wedding—though muumuus and Waikiki had played no part.

"No." She tried to think of something appealing and still keep the planning under the radar. "Maybe you could pretend you're planning a regular party. You could wear a pretty cocktail dress, have everything done more like a party, and then when the parents arrive, surprise! It's a wedding."

Kendall, who obviously had a stubborn streak a mile wide and perhaps not as creative a mind as Taylor, firmed her jaw and shook her head. She poked her index finger against the magazine so it made a snapping sound. "This is what I want."

White tulle and froth, pink roses and garlands and a four-tier wedding cake, those cherubic-looking flower girls. Taylor sighed in pure bliss. "You want a fairy-tale wedding."

"I know. It's hokey, but I can't help myself. I see pew bows and I get misty."

They both stared at that picture the way little girls stare at princess picture books. "Maybe you could hire this wedding party. No actual people could look this pretty."

"I know. I'm falling for a big fantasy wedding. And I'm an actuary," Kendall groaned.

"You're a romantic," Taylor corrected.

"Also totally out of luck if I don't keep this secret."

Taylor was thinking hard. She'd never met a party problem she couldn't fix. Never. "Once I put on a surprise birthday party for my h—boyfriend. He never knew a thing about it. If I could plan a surprise party for the man I was living with, surely we can plan a wedding without Dylan's parents finding out."

"How did you do it?"

"I set up this elaborate story that I was putting on a baby shower for a friend of ours. The minute I mentioned the words *baby shower* he stopped paying attention."

"I'm not trying to keep this from Dylan. It's his parents—"

She stopped when Taylor gasped and snapped her fingers as the obvious answer popped into her head. "What you need is a front person."

"Front person?"

"Sure. A fake. A stand-in. It's basic covert ops. We fool the FBI and the CIA by having a decoy bride. Omnimedia will be trickier, though."

Kendall started to laugh. "A decoy bride. I love it." She flipped through the magazine with a lot more enthusiasm. She opened to a page where her note read "Perfect dress!"

"See this dress? I want this dress, but I've been too scared even to try it on."

Taylor glanced at the magazine and thought that the simple ecru sheath dress with dainty tracings of lace would look stunning on Kendall. She nodded. "What you need is to plan a shopping trip with your wedding decoy. A friend who is getting married."

"I don't have any friends in the area. In fact, I don't know anyone who's getting married."

"You're being too literal. Find a friend who's willing to pretend to get married. Someone who's approximately the same size as you would be ideal." She stared at the wedding layout in the magazine and started figuring out the logistics in her head. "You pretend to be the bridesmaid or something. You go bride-dress shopping. You both disappear into the dressing room, but you, the secret bride, are the one who really tries on the gown."

Kendall looked as though she'd never, in all her years of calculating risks and retirement annuities and whatever it was that actuaries did, let her mind make such a creative leap. "Taylor, you are a genius."

"I know," she said with pride. "I told you, I'm great at stuff like this. Now all you need is a decoy bride."

The entire stack of magazines came up off the

floor and Kendall spread them all over the table like an extremely large and frilly poker deck. "Are you kidding me? I've already got a stand-in picked out."

"Really? That's great. Who?"

Kendall folded the open page and placed the magazine carefully into Taylor's lap. Her smile dimmed that of any of the pictured brides. "You."

CHAPTER NINE

"WHAT'S UP?" DYLAN ASKED, entering his motor home in time to hear Taylor make a bunch of groaning, spluttering, incoherent noises.

Hank followed. "Nothing," Taylor squeaked out.

"She's being modest," said Kendall, stretching her legs out in front of her. "She's about to save our lives. Or at least our wedding."

Dylan crossed to Kendall and kissed her, obviously such a habit that he didn't even think about it. "Thanks, Taylor," he said, pushing aside a stack of bridal magazines and sitting beside his fiancée.

"Cool," said Hank. Then he looked at the two women, obviously realizing that Taylor was less than thrilled with whatever was going on. He sat beside her and glanced at the magazine open and forgotten on her lap. "Nice dress. So, how's Taylor going to save you?" he asked Kendall.

Kendall glanced across at Taylor and Hank sitting side by side, sharing a bridal magazine, and she began to laugh. "Exactly the way you are going to save Dylan."

"I'm going to save Dylan? Sounds good. So long as it doesn't involve mouth-to-mouth or anything."

"Worse," Taylor managed to say. "It involves a tuxedo."

Hank glanced at the magazine, then at Dylan. Shook his head. "Not worse."

"Taylor is going to pretend to be getting married and I'll act the part of her bridesmaid. If you pretend you're marrying Taylor and Dylan's your best man, then Dy's parents will never know we're getting married until it's too late." Kendall beamed across the small space. "Taylor is so smart."

Taylor wasn't normally the quietest person in a crowd, but she couldn't seem to think of anything to say that wouldn't seem unfriendly, unhelpful and downright mean. A friend, albeit a new friend, was asking for her help, a little shopping-decoy time. It wasn't like Kendall was asking for a kidney. How could she say no? What possible reason would she give for not being willing to front as a bride?

Except the one reason she couldn't give.

That she'd done the bride thing once, and it hadn't worked out so well. She could only imagine the torment in store for her as she and Kendall shopped for everything from invitations to boutonnieres.

As Kendall fully explained Taylor's *brilliant* idea to the two men, she hoped that Hank would gag on the idea more loudly and directly than she had and save her butt for her.

But Hank, being Hank, who next to racing

seemed to love a good joke more than anything in the world, was laughing so hard the whole built-in couch was shaking.

Apparently, he wasn't going to refuse.

"But, Hank," she said, "what about your profile? As an up-and-coming driver, you're a celebrity, too. Won't the fans and media be a problem?"

"Not until I win a few races, get huge sponsorship deals with my face all over TV and billboards and have my face and buff bod plastered all over *People* magazine," he said, referring to Dylan's career rather than his own. Of course, all that would happen for him if she had anything to say about it, but she knew he was right. He was still pretty unrecognizable.

She tried another tack. "Are you sure you'll have time? With two racing schedules, I don't want you getting stressed out."

"Nah. It'll be fun."

"I think it's a great idea," Dylan said, obviously as excited as Kendall at the thought of actually setting a date.

"How tall are you, Taylor?" asked the bride.

With a sinking feeling of inevitability, she said, "Five six."

"I'm five five and a half." She smiled angelically. "Perfect."

"Really—"

"Dress size?"

"Six."

"Perfect again." She beamed. "This was absolutely meant to be. I can't believe you thought of such a great plan, Taylor."

She couldn't believe she hadn't stuck a fork in her eye. It would have been more fun than the ordeal ahead.

"So, honey," Hank said, giving Taylor his bad-little-boy grin and moving closer on the couch, "when's the day you're going to make me the happiest man in the world by becoming my wife?"

"The day after you send Denise and her Chihuahua home," she reminded him sweetly.

He looked a little guilty when she reminded him of his guest. "Right. I wonder where she is?"

"Last time I saw her she said something about shopping for a new bikini."

He perked up a little. "I better go find her."

"For her dog."

His face fell. "Oh, man. One good thing about this fake wedding gig, I won't have to invite women like Denise to any more races."

Alarm skittered through Taylor's nervous system. "What do you mean?"

"What do you think I mean? If we're engaged, I'm not going to bring some other woman to the races, *honey.*"

"This is a secret, Hank. It has to be. I mean it. I won't do it if anyone in this room tells a single soul about our pretend engagement."

Kendall and Dylan glanced at her with curiosity. Hank seemed put out. "What's wrong with being engaged to me? Aren't I a good catch?"

She bit her lip. "Of course you are. It's just that—" A vision of Mike's face rose up before her. She couldn't imagine how he'd take the news and she couldn't stand the idea of him ever finding out about this stunt. She didn't think his reaction would be quite as jocular as Hank's.

"I'm not good-looking enough, I bet. You've been spending too much time with Dylan and Carl."

"I think you're very nice-looking," she said, feeling like she'd fallen into choppy seas with no life raft. What if Hank's feelings got hurt and he raced badly tomorrow? How could she ever live with herself?

"Maybe I'm not rich enough." He looked at her sadly and shook his head. "I didn't peg you for a mercenary woman."

"Of course I don't care about your money. Think of my position. I work for you. I could never hold up my head as a professional again if we were linked romantically."

Hank looked less than impressed. "You work for Winfield Racing, not for me."

"I'm five years older than you."

Hank glanced at her from under ridiculously long lashes. "What's five years when you're in love?"

"Love? I—" Only now did she see the telltale muscle that bulged under his jaw. "You jerk! You were teasing me."

She thought, not for the first time, that she'd have been better prepared for this job if she'd had a younger brother.

She rose, did exactly what she imagined she'd have done if one of her imaginary brothers got her going. She punched him in the shoulder. Not entirely gently.

He was laughing so hard he nearly fell onto the floor. "Hey, that's my steering arm."

"It's your right arm. All you have to do out there on the track is turn left."

"Remind me never to make you really mad," he said.

"Come on, nobody's going to rat you out. It'll be fun. Like playing a practical joke on the whole world."

A practical joke that could too easily backfire if news spread.

"You don't have to do this, Taylor," Kendall said, suddenly looking concerned. "I shouldn't have assumed…"

When Taylor saw the way the glow of excitement faded from Kendall's cheeks, she felt like a worm. What was the matter with her? The switcheroo had been her idea and it was a great one. So long as the supposed engagement between her and Hank remained between the four of them and a few wedding businesses why would news spread?

"Of course I'll do it. I want to." She forced a smile and lied through her teeth. "Hank's right. It'll be fun."

"What is the date?" Hank asked.

"We have to fit in with the racing schedule, obviously," Kendall said, glancing at Dy, who was thumbing through a bridal mag. "But there's a week off in July that would be perfect."

"July's good," Dylan agreed. "Not much time for a honeymoon, but we can charter a buddy's boat in the Caribbean between races."

"Perfect."

July. Five months. She could do this, she told herself. It was for a good cause. What could possibly go wrong?

Hank pulled out a pair of aviator sunglasses and rose. "I guess I'd better go find Denise." In qualifying he'd had a good enough time to let him start in fourteenth position tomorrow, which she thought was fantastic for a rookie. She could feel how much more relaxed he was. Still, it was his first big race tomorrow. He might tease her mercilessly, but she still needed to smooth his path as much as she possibly could.

"Why don't I go find her?"

She rose and they said goodbye to Kendall and Dylan and left the motor home.

"You don't have to do that."

"I don't mind. In the meantime, you can go over your media messages for tomorrow."

They'd practiced answers to all the obvious questions and he was a naturally smart guy. He'd do fine.

"Yes, ma'am."

He'd had a session already today with his performance coach. He'd finished respectably in the

NASCAR Busch Series race, which had to have let off some steam, and he had a good starting position tomorrow. Everything else would come down to timing, skill and pure, blind luck.

Maybe she wasn't a performance coach, but she was going to do her best to boost his confidence every chance she got. She turned to him and said, "And pay special attention to the messages we came up with for when you win."

Then she patted his arm and went off to find Denise. She didn't think it would take long since she doubted there could be many places that sold Chihuahua clothes.

TAYLOR FLASHED HER credentials to the guard and walked into the Daytona track media center. On the wall to her left was a display of press releases. She checked, and sure enough, there was one of hers, a full backgrounder on Hank Excellent.

Sadly, there were far too many copies still left waiting to be snatched up into eager reporters' hands.

Outside the main media room was a scattering of tables. A wall-mounted TV showed racing coverage, and a dozen or so people were sitting chatting, sipping coffee. Soon, she imagined she'd know most of them, but for now they were all strangers.

She entered the media room and experienced a thrill. This was a world she knew so well. There was something about a large room full of people writing copy that made her fingers itch for a keyboard.

About half the workstations were occupied. They were set up in rows. At the front of the room was a table covered with a cloth imprinted with the NASCAR logo. Three mikes were mounted. This, she knew, was where the three top-placing drivers would come for post-race interviews.

She'd seen the spot many times on television, but it was fun to see it live. At the back of the room was another raised platform for TV cameras to set up.

She walked up the first row, reading the cardboard tent cards that designated which reporter sat where, a bit like place cards at a fancy dinner party. Or a wedding, she thought, her bright mood dimming slightly.

A big part of her job would be to work with these people, pitching them stories about Hank and feeding them press releases and information. She wanted to meet as many reporters as she could and had deliberately chosen a time she judged to be not too busy when they might have time to chat with her for a few minutes.

Most of them were only too happy to pause for a minute or two, swap business cards and get to know her a little bit. One print journalist pulled up a short piece he'd written about Hank that was going in the next issue of the paper. An online columnist, a young woman with short blond hair and a happy-face smile, promised to send her a list of the best places to eat on the circuit.

These people spent as much time on the road as

the drivers and their teams, but without being accorded the same luxuries. No helicopter or private jets whisked the reporters home. They had to fight the traffic week after week to and from the track, put up with the vagaries of commercial air travel and keep feeding the blogs, online news sites and the traditional media.

She asked one reporter when he got a day off and he snorted and replied, "What's that?" Still, she could tell he wouldn't change his job for anything.

She'd managed to talk briefly with about half the reporters present when she glanced up, sensing rather than hearing the main door open. In walked Mike Lundquist. He had his jacket thrown over his shoulder and a notebook in one hand. His gaze came unerringly to hers and she saw the infinitesimal pause in his step before he continued into the room. Her heart did that irritating jumpy thing it always did when she saw him. She suspected it always would. Maybe once you'd been as close to someone as she'd been to Mike, you could never break the habit of an emotional response. Unless there was some kind of twelve-step program to break the addiction. She'd have to look into it when she got time.

Mike didn't come near her, but sent her a slight nod and walked straight over to his spot while she went back to introducing herself. By the time she got to his row, Mike was tapping away with his own unique style of keyboarding. He used the middle three fingers of each hand so his fingers always looked as though they were in a hurry to catch up with the keys he was pounding.

"Still haven't learned how to type, I see," she said, coming up behind him.

He didn't raise his head but kept tapping on his laptop. "Still haven't learned not to interrupt a writer in the heat of creation, I see."

She leaned down so she could read over his shoulder. "The Perfect NASCAR Fan, yep, that will change the course of journalism as we know it." She realized she'd made a terrible mistake when a wave of nostalgia threatened to topple her to the floor. The way she was bent over him, they were almost cheek to cheek. Closer than they'd been in more than a year. His smell was so familiar, the scents of his soap—which smelled like plain soap because she knew he hated scented cleansers of any kind—and shampoo—the same kind he'd been using ever since she'd known him. His cheeks were dark with emerging stubble, and this close she could see that two of his lower eyelashes had crossed.

Something else was going on, too. She knew he was as aware of her closeness as she was aware of his. Even though he never moved, and the frenetic tapping continued, she felt the buzz of connection, irritatingly strong still, between them.

"What do you want?" he suddenly snapped, as though he couldn't stand having her so close to him for one more second. It was the release she needed, and she straightened, flopping into the spare chair beside him.

"I'm going around introducing myself to the media," she said, spouting her well-thought-out introductory line.

He flicked her a glance, dark and dangerous. "We've met."

He went back to typing.

"You spelled *approximate* wrong," she said sweetly. "There are two *p*'s."

He dropped his hands and turned to her. "Okay. You have my full attention. My name's Mike Lundquist. I'm a NASCAR reporter." He held out his hand, the second time he'd done so since they'd bumped into each other in Charlotte. Mockery danced in his eyes.

And, for the second time, she shook his hand, determined that before long he was going to be the one begging her for attention. Just let Hank win a few races and she'd wipe the I'm-still-a-reporter-and-you're-not expression off his face.

"You keep an eye on my driver," she said to him. "You just keep an eye on him."

She rose and turned away, but not before she heard him say, "On him and his cute PR manager."

Deciding the dignified response was none at all, she continued with her tour of the media center, ending with a pocketful of business cards and a pretty good idea of who was most receptive to stories about a relatively unknown rookie driver.

And who wasn't.

She'd as good as promised Mike that Hank was

going to be worth watching this season. She had no idea why she'd done anything so foolish, except that he'd annoyed her.

No, she thought, as she made her way back out into the sunshine and meandering streams of race fans, her comment was based on more than that. Some instinct.

She recognized in Hank a streak of competitive steel that perhaps was more obvious to her because she'd competed so often herself. She'd never been a serious athlete, but she'd known plenty who were, and she'd come to recognize a certain indefinable something, some quality that went beyond skill or competitiveness. She supposed it was a kind of magic. She didn't have a crystal ball, but she knew one thing. Hank had that magic.

CHAPTER TEN

SUNDAY WAS A PERFECT DAY for racing. Sunny but not too hot, the sky so clear and blue there was no danger of rain, and the air shifted with only a slight breeze. She hoped that a perfect day was a good omen for Hank's first NASCAR NEXTEL Cup race.

She was so nervous she could barely stand still. She felt as proud of Hank as if he was her brother and so nervous she thought she might throw up.

Her driver was fortunately made of sterner stuff. If he was nervous, it didn't show. He stood proudly in his brand-new uniform with the name of the chain of hardware stores that was sponsoring him prominently identified.

"How are you feeling?" she asked him.

He grinned at her and she could see the excitement shining in his eyes. "I feel good," he said. "Real good." He glanced around as though he couldn't believe that he was here. "Today is going to be a great day." He wasn't bouncing or twitching. She thought he was instinctively conserving energy.

They made their way to the staging area where

drivers were milling around, each with his PR manager. Fans watched from the perimeter.

Carl Edwards caught sight of Hank and immediately walked over.

"How you doing?" he asked Hank.

"I'm doing good. Not too nervous." He stood there for a second and asked, "Do you have any advice for the rookie?"

"Yeah. Drive fast. But not faster than me."

They laughed and even that little release helped dim Taylor's stress level. She took a quick glance around and thought that most of the PR managers looked more tense than their drivers.

"Really, what I would say is just, you know, enjoy the moment. I'm guessing you've dreamed of this day since you were a little kid."

Hank nodded. She could picture him hanging around cars as a little guy, watching races, finally getting a chance to try a cart, and falling in love with the sport.

"There's a lot more guys who dream of going out there than will ever get the chance. You have to go out there and drive like you mean it. Drive with your heart and your guts. All your dreams are right out there. Keep your focus and—" he shrugged, looked up at the sky as though for inspiration "—do what has to be done."

"Okay."

"What we do is amazing. Right?" Carl looked

like he'd pumped himself up with his pep talk. "This is so cool."

"It sure is. I've been practicing my back flips, in case I win."

Carl treated them to his toothy grin. "Stick to something you can handle. Like a cartwheel."

The picture of Hank in his blue-and-yellow uniform turning cartwheels was so ridiculous she had to laugh.

He appeared to take the suggestion seriously. "Think that's too flashy? Maybe I should stick to one of them, what do you call them? Somersaults."

Carl gave him a mock punch. "You're going to be okay."

Then the drivers were being introduced. She heard Hank's name called and felt another swell of pride. This was it. While he made his introductory lap, she made her way to the team's spot on pit road.

The air was buzzing with excitement. She took a moment to look up at the stands and enjoy the spectacle of more than 165,000 fans all set for one of the premier events in racing. The stands were a sea of color. Fans sported racing gear, most of which was in bold primary colors. It was a rainbow of caps, jackets, T-shirts. Even their coolers matched.

Hank arrived, looking pretty colorful himself in his blue-and-yellow uniform. He stood by his car chatting with his crew chief and Denise, who looked gorgeous in a blue tank top and curve-hugging yellow jeans. Her long dark hair shone and she was clearly loving the moment. Fortunately, Cutie Pie was currently snoozing in Hank's motor home since Denise had been afraid the engine noise would scare him.

Photographers were everywhere, snapping photos from every conceivable angle. Hank, like most of the drivers, did his best to pretend he didn't notice.

As drivers walked by, they'd give him a good-natured shove, or mumble something that she assumed meant good luck in some incomprehensible sports-guy speak.

Hank talked to his crew chief and Taylor was thrilled to see a broadcaster walk by for a quick interview.

"How do you think you're going to do out there today?" he asked. A no-brainer question and one she'd prepared him for.

"I'm going to do my best. I've got a great team behind me, a company I'm proud to race for and sponsors and fans who believe in me." He broke into his infectious grin. "I have to tell you, and everybody out there who's rooting for me today, that I feel ready for this."

Denise gave him a big hug and then was escorted to sit on top of the pit box to watch the race. Taylor doubted she'd stay there long, but she'd done exactly what Hank had wanted her to do. She'd looked gorgeous, sent him off on his first race in style. And, Taylor thought with relief, after the race, she'd be flying on to Miami for a modeling assignment, meaning she was no longer Taylor's problem.

Taylor stood by while he climbed into his car, put in ear plugs, pulled on his helmet and plugged it in. She wished she had time to go for a run as she watched him strapping in, putting the steering wheel on—getting ready to go.

When she heard the words, "Gentlemen, start your engines," she thought she might hyperventilate. This was it. Not only Hank's rookie race, but hers.

She walked with the crew chief to the pits and took her place behind the war wagon, stationing herself at a monitor.

For the next four hours, she'd be taking notes on everything going on. She'd have to write a recap after the race for sponsors, fans, media and Hank and the team. At the same time, she was looking for something interesting to give to one of the four pit reporters who would in turn feed any story nuggets to the broadcasters in the sky.

She remembered Mike's advice to make good friends with them and could see how that could be important.

She had notepads and pens, and her own headset so she could hear the conversation between Hank and his crew chief. She had a good supply of cola to see her through. She was ready.

She imagined the three commentators in the booth and hoped she could find something to feed them. Already the pit reporters were running up and down pit road with a camera crew following them.

She watched from her monitor as the pace cars pulled away and the race began.

She scribbled furiously, which in a way helped keep her tension to a manageable level. Hank was holding steady but not trying anything clever, she noticed. She heard the ongoing conversation between him and his crew chief and she got the feeling the older man was a calming influence.

Hank's spotter was up high, looking down. She liked to think of him as Hank's personal guardian angel.

The first half of the race passed in a blur. Hank moved up so he was in the bottom of the top ten, juggling between six and nine. If he ended the race in the top ten she knew he'd have to feel successful.

There was a caution called and Hank took the opportunity to pit. All four tires were changed and she finally had something newsworthy for the pit reporter. She ran after him with a note that said, "cut tire."

Next thing she knew, the camera crew was upon them. "That caution came out at the right time for rookie driver Hank Mission," the reporter announced. He held up the tire that she'd marked with chalk to show the developing hole. "Yeah, it was a great time. You can see where there's a gash of some kind right here in the circled area. Hank got in before it blew up. I guess you call that beginner's luck."

As the race wore on she wrote a lot of little notes with cryptic messages like "four tires, half round of wedge out" or "took a half pound of air out of front tire."

Hank sounded strong and confident, even when he was complaining, "It's pushing like a truck."

And all the time she charted his progress. Her notebook was full of things like: lap thirteen, sixth place, three seconds back, lap forty, caution. She'd need these notes to write up her report which she'd send to all the sponsors, put up on the Web site and send to Hank's fan club. She'd also send a post-race report to all media by e-mail.

During the pre-race media madness, she'd seen the big-name drivers getting swarmed. Her driver wasn't, but he certainly wasn't ignored, either. His was a new face and that alone generated some interest.

He'd handled himself well, remembered to say all the things she'd taught him and added a big dose of his own charm and youthful energy. If, today, he stayed in the top ten, she had good reason to think he'd get a lot more interest. She listened to the dialogue between Hank and his spotter. They weren't exactly chatty. There was a lot of silence punctuated with bursts of information on what was ahead and behind of the driver.

Hank still appeared well placed. Of course, there were almost two hours to go yet. Anything could happen. All she wanted was for him to make it all the way through his first race and not to come in last.

She knew that someone had to come in last, but she didn't want it to be Hank, not on his debut.

Then, one of those events that make racing so utterly unpredictable and exciting happened. The car running third clipped the side wall on Turn Three and took the fourth-place car out with him.

Hank was suddenly no longer sixth. He was fourth. The possibility of him placing in the top five was very real.

For a full ten minutes she forgot to take a single note as she watched her monitor, transfixed.

Anything could happen.

CHAPTER ELEVEN

MIKE SAT HUNCHED OVER HIS laptop in the media center at Daytona, probably as stunned as anyone. Rows of workstations allowed the journalists and photojournalists to write and file material. Outside he could hear convivial laughter from those not currently sweating over a deadline, who could hang out over coffee and doughnuts in the main foyer, where most of the socializing took place.

He imagined most of them were talking about the same thing he was currently typing about—the incredible second-place finish of rookie driver Hank Mission.

Incredible didn't begin to describe the accomplishment. To finish the race without humiliating himself would have been an achievement. Mike couldn't imagine what kind of talent, smarts and coolness under pressure was hidden under that flop of hair and the "aw, shucks, it weren't nothin'" attitude.

He'd watched the race from the press box that overlooked the start/finish line. As races go, it wasn't the most dramatic, or it hadn't been until Hank Mission had made his mark on Daytona.

Up front was the raised stage area where the top three drivers were required to appear after a race for a media scrum Q & A.

Hank Mission was the story today. And what a story. He'd taken the decision not to pit late in the race and luck had swooped down and kissed him full on the lips. Shortly after most of the teams had pitted, a caution was called and Mission saved probably ten or twelve seconds. It put him up in the top three, and after that he'd been the story of the race, swapping the lead a few times but never faltering. In fact, there'd been a while when it looked like he'd do the unthinkable and win his first race.

Luck, mechanics, driving skill, a pit crew that had worked flawlessly and with blind determination; everything had aligned for the rookie driver, and Mike was curious to see how the normally shy-seeming, soft-spoken driver would handle himself riding the rush of his amazing accomplishment.

So, it seemed, did everyone else. The chatter outside died down as every reporter and photographer in the place made their way into the media room. The three top-placed drivers walked in a few minutes later, pausing to acknowledge the congratulations. This wasn't hard news reporting or a presidential scrum. The men and women who covered NASCAR got to know one another and the drivers, and Mike knew most everyone in the media was happy to imagine a new face in Victory Lane, not only for a fresh story, but also because most of them genuinely liked the new guy.

The three drivers made their way to the front, but Mike's attention was snagged by the woman who slipped into the room behind her driver. Taylor looked radiant, he thought, as well she might. If he knew her, and he did, she'd be almost as excited as Hank himself.

Her eyes scanned the room quickly, her gaze hovering over him but never landing, and then she made certain not to glance his way again. Her obvious avoidance shouldn't have annoyed him, but it did. They'd been married. As close as two people could be. Now she couldn't even look at him? Okay, so maybe he hadn't handled things as well as he could have when their marriage hit a rough patch, but had she done any better? Maybe he'd withdrawn from conflict, as the one counselor he'd been crazy enough to see had suggested, but he'd only gone as far as work or a buddy's place for a poker evening. So, maybe he'd retreated a little, but his lovely wife had run screaming into the night as fast and as far as she could. He'd gone to work more than he should, but she'd high-tailed it to frickin' Australia.

He looked at her, knowing he was safe to do so since her eyes were so firmly and determinedly turned away from his direction. The trouble when you'd been intimate with someone was that you never forgot. As hard as he tried, he couldn't see

Taylor as Hank's PR manager. He saw her as his wife. As the woman who got all his jokes.

He remembered that about her from the first day she'd walked into the newsroom, young and fresh and still full of the idealism of journalism school. She was too blond, too cute, too preppy. He'd assumed the managing editor had got lost in her green eyes and given the cub reporter position to a gal who didn't have enough toughness in her to cover a student council meeting. Then he'd cracked some stupid joke and she'd laughed. The sound had amazed him. It was like old, smoky malt whiskey pouring out of a pop bottle—unexpected, attractive, seductive.

She'd caught all his references, whether to sports or current events or obscure historical facts. Like many reporters, he was a trivia buff. Turned out she was, too. In the Pacific Northwest where the top sports were baseball, football and basketball, it turned out he and Taylor were the only two NASCAR fans at the paper.

Now he thought of it, NASCAR had brought them together. He didn't believe in dating a coworker, it was just a bad idea on every level. So he hadn't thought of it as a date when he and Taylor met at a local sports bar to watch the races on a Sunday afternoon. Naturally, they loved different drivers. She tended toward the younger daredevils while he put his money behind the seasoned guys, the ones who knew every inch of every track, who'd seen years of action and could read a car the way a palm reader interprets an open hand.

First they bet over who'd buy the beer and burgers. Then one amazing day, after he'd had more of the former than the latter and his courage was high, he'd suggested whoever won had to cook the other dinner. She had a way of looking at him that suggested she'd heard all his lines before, knew his moves as well as he did. The idea that she was on to him kind of turned him on. The fact that she was into him turned him on even more.

When she stared at him for a long moment, and then agreed, he knew he'd won. It didn't matter who cooked the dinner, what mattered was that they were moving on to the next stage.

He should have been nervous. He never got personal with anybody at work. It was a bad policy. Bad, bad, bad. But for some reason everything seemed different with Taylor. She felt like a friend more than a woman he was interested in, but of course, he was fooling himself. He was more interested in her than he ever remembered being in any woman.

He remembered the current that flowed between them, unspoken but strong, as they watched the race that day. The knowledge that if she cooked dinner for him or he cooked dinner for her, they were moving from buddies to—well, there were a lot of directions this could go, but a man had his hopes.

Within three months they were married.

Three months. He scowled down at his keyboard while the race winners got themselves settled up front. Three months. What had they known about each other really? She laughed at his jokes. They both loved NASCAR. He was a better cook than she was. She was the only woman he could go to bed wanting and wake up wanting a little bit more.

Sometimes she made him angry, but she never irritated him, which was rare in his experience. Was that enough to build a lifetime on?

Clearly not.

An image flashed into his mind of her in front of the full-length mirror, turning this way and that, trying to convince herself that her pregnancy was showing. She was maybe seven weeks at that point and her belly looked as flat to him as ever, but he lied and said he definitely saw a bump there.

She was still lithe and lean, he thought as he watched Taylor position herself to the side but well within Hank's line of vision. The driver needed that point of contact with someone he knew and trusted. Yet it annoyed him to see Hank looking to Mike's ex-wife for reassurance before his first big media scrum.

He glanced between the two of them. Taylor was beaming, as excited about the win as her driver. It was obvious those two had a rapport going. Which was good, of course.

Hank was considered a pretty funny guy. Mike wondered if Taylor got all his jokes.

If Mike were a driver, he'd try to win a race for

her, but he wasn't a driver. He was a newspaper columnist, and no matter how inspired and thrilling his commentary on NASCAR, he doubted it would be the stuff to win a stubborn woman's heart. For the second time.

He wasn't a poet or a songwriter; he couldn't even write short stories or a novel. He had a couple hundred of pages of drek to prove it.

Maybe, whatever it was that would unlock her heart was something he didn't have at all, he thought grimly as things got started and he reluctantly turned his attention to Hank Mission, now fielding questions.

"How does it feel to place second in your first official season?"

The driver's grin was sure and slow. "It feels nice. Real nice."

And they were off. All three took questions, but Hank was the obvious story.

"How were the other drivers out there?"

"Some guys gave me some slack." He grinned. "Maybe they won't do that again. We had a car that was fast, and my team really pulled together."

He talked about track conditions, strategic decisions that had made a difference, and he transferred a lot of credit to his crew chief and his pit crew. Nice going, Hank, Mike thought. Then he glanced at his ex-wife, who was watching Hank with clear, careful eyes. Or nice going, Taylor, he thought.

Hank was talking from his heart, but he was

talking well and mentioning everybody he needed to. Taylor had been in the media long enough to know all about sound bites and image. She'd obviously coached Hank to get him ready for this day. It had come sooner than anybody had imagined, but good for her for thinking ahead. Good for Hank for listening to her. He was media-ready.

Mike focused on Hank's words, on doing his job, writing his column, but Taylor remained in his mind, there but not there, like a familiar and comforting scent. She was wearing jeans and a Winfield Racing golf shirt, but he got hints of her athletic body when she moved around.

When the top three were done with the Q & A, they left. As Hank headed down the aisle beside the workstations toward the exit, he put a hand over Taylor's shoulder and gave her neck a squeeze. Mike felt as though he'd taken a bullet somewhere soft and painful. He couldn't look away, and so he didn't miss the way Taylor leaned into her boy and gave him one of her wide, mischievous smiles.

Taylor and Hank? The idea revolted him. She was working for the guy, she had five years on him; Mike hadn't seen it coming. But the worst part, of course, was that if she was seeing Hank, then she wasn't thinking about her ex-hubby. So why was it that her ex-hubby couldn't stop thinking about her?

NASCAR drivers have incredible reflexes and Mike had noticed that a lot of times their senses seemed heightened, too, so it almost wasn't a surprise when Hank paused at the door, turned his head and returned Mike's stare. Neither of them acknowledged each other in any way, just locked gazes for a second, and then the driver turned, still with his hand on Taylor's shoulder, and left.

Mike wanted to haul Hank Mission out of the media center and go a few rounds, knowing he'd get himself pounded into the asphalt for his trouble. Hank was a young buck of an athlete, while he was...not—even when he was bothering to work out. Taylor used to like his teddy bear build, or at least she'd pretended to. Seemed her tastes had changed.

Turning back to his computer, he contemplated eviscerating his opponent in print, where he did have muscle, but he dropped the idea before his hands hit the keyboard. If only Hank had come across arrogant and full of himself, had taken all the credit for the second-place finish, Mike would have had a fighting chance. However, Hank Mission was a good guy who'd handled his first win with a lot of class, and that meant Mike couldn't use the only weapon he was any good with. Sometimes playing fair sucked.

TAYLOR FELT THE TENSION in her shoulders ease as she got Hank out of the media room. She'd had the double stress of watching Hank handle himself at that all-important first post-race media conference, while at the same time knowing Mike was there in the room, watching her, judging her, probably based on how well Hank performed.

"You did great in there," she said when they left the media center and jumped back into the golf cart that would return them to Hank's motor home.

"I remembered about a tenth of the things you told me to say," he admitted, "but the press went pretty easy on me."

Their driver scooted them through the organized commotion of teams packing up to head out again. Some jubilant, some not. Outside the restricted area, she could see streams of fans, sporting the clothing and chair pads and drink cup holders of their NASCAR heroes, heading out to their vehicles.

"You remembered all the important talking points. Thanking the sponsors and remembering to emphasize the whole team pulling together."

"Well, it's true."

"People liked your modesty. Even the cynical reporters."

Hank shrugged his shoulders. He might be trying to play it cool, but the excitement was still vibrating the air all around him. "It's like my mama always told me. Everybody likes a winner, but nobody likes a braggart."

"Pretty smart mama."

"I make it a point to surround myself with smart women," he said, sending her the crafty glance she was beginning to know and distrust. "So," Hank said, "what's going on with you and Mike Lundquist?"

She nearly fell off the cart and into the road. "What do you mean?"

"I don't know, but we were walking out and I felt like I had to watch my back all of a sudden. I turned around and Mike was staring at me. He didn't look happy."

"Maybe he had money staked on another driver."

"Maybe he has a thing for you and didn't like seeing my arm around you."

She thought of all the lies she could tell and for a second contemplated spinning one. But Hank wasn't only her employer, he was becoming a friend. She owed him honesty. If she couldn't tell him the truth, she couldn't lie to him. So she said, "It's complicated, but I don't think it's anything you need to worry about."

"Complicated, like you're seeing a guy who could mess with my career?"

"No. I'm not 'seeing' Mike Lundquist. Trust me. It's nothing."

"Maybe it's nothing to you, but I'm telling you, that guy's got a major crush on one of us."

She laughed. "I think you're safe. In fact, I think we both are."

She could feel Hank looking at her but wouldn't return his gaze. "If you say so," he said.

Winfield Racing had its own plane waiting, and it was a jovial group who boarded. Taylor was about to start writing her most exciting post-race report when she glanced up to find Mike coming toward her.

Damn it, in all the excitement she'd forgotten all

about his profile, or that he'd be flying back with
them. He had a jocular few words with Gordon
Winfield. She couldn't hear the words, but they were
all but backslapping each other. How nauseating.

However, since it was Gordon who wanted Mike
to do the interview, she guessed she was going to
have to suck it up and let him.

There was a tiny table and seating area in the passenger cabin, and he settled the three of them there.
Hank was still riding the high of his great result. She
was starting to feel the effects of the tension she'd
been under trying to make sure everything was successful.

She was ready to crash into bed and sleep for a
couple of days.

Instead, she stuck her smile back on, not caring
that Mike would see how fake it was. He had to
know she didn't want to do this.

Mike had clearly put whatever bad feelings he had
for Hank behind him. His congratulations sounded
sincere, and the fact that he congratulated her, too,
for helping Hank sound so media savvy, helped him
win a brownie point or two in his favor.

He used a small tape recorder, something he
didn't often do, and it sat between them on the table,
reminding her that this was strictly business.

Mike sat back, his notebook out, and said to Hank,
"Tell me the whole story."

Hank did, reliving the day, something he was obviously still processing himself. She loved his enthu-

siasm and the way Mike let him talk, only interpolating the odd question. A few times, Hank's accent got so thick she could barely understand a word, but Mike seemed to have no trouble.

She watched him taking notes, showing an interest in the young driver. Mike's eyelashes were ridiculously long for a man. And thick. She'd always envied him those lashes. She didn't realize she was staring until Mike glanced up and caught her at it. There was a second when she couldn't look away and they stayed locked in some silent communication that was deeper than words.

He looked away first, giving his attention back to Hank, and she carefully kept her gaze on the table until pulled into the conversation, when Mike asked Hank, "How do you find Taylor to work with?"

It seemed like a personal question, not something he'd be printing in a newspaper or an online blog, but Hank answered readily enough. "She's great. Smart, organized, takes no crap." He shot a devilish look at Mike. "Easy on the eyes, too."

Once more Mike's gaze flicked to hers. "Yeah. I noticed."

"Oh, stop it," she said. "If you don't have any need of me, I'll go—"

"I do. Have need of you."

There was a pause that was so full of meaning you could stir it with a spoon.

She crossed her arms. Then, realizing how defensive that must look, deliberately relaxed them by her sides. "Ask your questions, then. We'll be in Charlotte soon."

"As a woman working in the sport, how do you like NASCAR?"

"I love it." She thought for a second about some of the people she'd met, especially the women. "There's a nineteen-year-old I know named Lisa. She races stock cars and her dream is to win at Daytona. It's only a matter of time before a female driver makes it to the top of the NASCAR NEXTEL Cup Series."

"But right now it's all guys."

"Sure. But it's an exciting time for the sport. I talk to women fans a lot and they are as passionate as men. I think for us we are more inclined to have favorite drivers, we root more easily for individuals than teams." She shrugged. "I don't know. That's what it feels like."

He nodded. "Do you have any racing background?"

He knew this, of course, but she supposed that it was an expected question and one he needed to ask. Her throat tightened a little as she answered. "Yes. My dad loved racing. We used to watch them together. A couple of times he took me to see races live. My mom was never interested, so it was our special thing." She glanced at Hank, who must wonder why she was getting misty-eyed over her memories. "He died last year. I wish he could have been there today."

"He would have loved it," Mike said.

"I'm sorry," Hank said. He glanced curiously between her and Mike, and she thought again that he hid a lot of sharp insights inside that country-boy façade.

CHAPTER TWELVE

TAYLOR COULD NOT IMAGINE a worse way to spend her Tuesday afternoon than to go wedding-dress shopping.

She was exhausted from the weekend of racing, had spent Monday writing a race recap for the sponsors and her media distribution list, spent a good part of the day with Hank organizing media and promotional opportunities and updating his schedule. After his big finish in Daytona, she could barely keep up with the requests.

Her driver was hot, which was great. It also meant that she was working twice as hard as usual.

She did not have time to help Dylan and Kendall with their wedding. However, Dylan was a teammate of Hank's and a friend, and she knew that by helping Dylan and Kendall she was also helping the team.

But did it have to be wedding-dress shopping? Couldn't they have started with something easy, like invitations?

They were meeting at a bridal shop and then going for lunch where, knowing Kendall, Taylor would be subjected to a detailed plan complete with timeline, itinerary, budget analysis and delegation chart. More than ever, she wished she'd kept her big mouth shut and her bright ideas about a bride decoy to herself.

She dressed in what she hoped would look like prospective-bride wear. A cotton dress that was easy to pull on and off, white sandals and—mostly because she knew Kendall and she would be sharing a change room—her prettiest underwear.

Traffic was light and she headed down I-85, reaching uptown Charlotte in less then thirty minutes. After finding parking, she strolled to the first boutique on the list Kendall had e-mailed her, complete with map directions, and located the bridal shop with no trouble at all. Foot traffic was light, and as she reached the shop she saw a familiar figure walking toward her. Without any conscious thought, she kept her pace steady so she'd passed the bridal boutique by the time she and Mike came face-to-face.

He looked as awkward bumping into her as she felt bumping into him. He was less scruffy than usual, she noted. His dark hair was neat, he was clean-shaven. He wore his usual blazer and jeans, but instead of a T-shirt, he wore an actual dress shirt and his loafers looked polished. For him, this was about as formal as she'd ever seen him.

"Hey, Taylor," he said. "Day off?"

"Yes. I'm just…" She scanned the vicinity rapidly. "I'm on my way to the sports-equipment store over there. I need some new runners."

He inspected the storefront and nodded. "That's a good place." As if he bought running shoes and sports equipment weekly. "I'm, uh, I'm meeting Dylan. We're going to shoot some pool."

"Okay. Have fun."

"Yeah, see you."

He headed on past and she crossed the street and jogged to the sports store. She entered, dodged through the racks of tracksuits, rounded a display of water bottles, and gave a cursory glance to the rows and rows of shoes, which she gazed at with the same longing Kendall had given to the dresses in the bridal magazines.

Reluctantly, she turned down an offer to fit her for the pair of cross-trainers she was salivating over, promising herself she'd come back later if there was time.

Then, deciding that Mike had had long enough to get to the pool hall, she moved to the front of the store. She peeked out the window just in case, but sure enough there was no sign of him.

Close call, she thought as she slipped on a pair of dark sunglasses before heading once more for the bridal boutique.

Feeling like an undercover agent, she skulked back up the road and looked both ways before slipping into the store.

A taxi pulled up outside before she'd even closed the door behind her and Kendall jumped out, looked neither right nor left, until she was inside, too.

"Hi," she said, in a bright, clear voice. "How is the bride-to-be?"

"Pretty excited," Taylor said, faking a *lucky me, I'm getting married* smile.

"Well, let's get started," said her friend. Kendall pretended to assess Taylor. "I'm seeing something simple. Elegant. Not a lot of frills. What do you see?"

"It's amazing," Taylor said, rolling her eyes so only Kendall could see her. "I think we have exactly the same taste."

Kendall raised one eyebrow. "That's why you picked me for your bridesmaid."

"May I help you?" a salesclerk asked. The woman was smooth, polished, obviously gauging their seriousness.

Taylor felt a nudge from Kendall and sprang into action. "Yes. I'm getting married." Funny how the words wanted to choke her. As if. She wondered if she was bringing bad luck on Kendall even being part of this charade, but there wasn't much she could do about it now. Maybe if she resolutely refused to think of her own disastrous marriage while she was helping Kendall, her bad-wedding karma couldn't infect a perfectly healthy relationship.

"Congratulations," the woman said. "When is the big day?"

"Oh," she muttered. "The big day." She turned to Kendall. "I swear if my head wasn't attached to my body...do you remember what we decided?"

Kendall gave her imitation of a girlish giggle. "That's why you have me as your bridesmaid. July. You picked July."

"Right. There's something about a summer wedding." Her wedding had been in February, so at least she didn't have additional memories of being a summer bride.

"Wonderful. You've got some time, but not enough to waste. There's quite a variety of styles to choose from. Were you looking for a traditional gown or something more modern?"

"I'm thinking something sleek and elegant," she said, parroting Kendall's words.

"Excellent choice. You're so slim. The simple elegance will be lovely on you." Taylor let the saleswoman and her "bridesmaid" make their suggestions while trying to appear suitably enthusiastic. In fact, she'd worn a dress to her own wedding that she picked up in half an hour at the boutique in the hotel where they were staying in Hawaii.

She and Mike had gone for a week's holiday to Maui after they'd been together all of three months.

It was a midwinter getaway to the sun, that's all. She'd intended to surf, snorkel, swim and relax with the boyfriend who made her laugh and was as much her friend as her lover.

Every day there were at least two weddings on the beach at their hotel, sometimes they were uninvited spectators at as many as four ceremonies. With a lot of time on their hands and a lot of mai tais in their systems, and an insatiable love of all sports, they'd taken to scoring each marriage effort.

Points were awarded for dresses, groom attire, bouquets and creativity. Bonus points automatically awarded for bare feet, a headdress that wasn't a veil and any flower unavailable in a florist shop. If any piece of greenery, clothing or décor ended up whipped by the wind and swept away by the waves, it carried an instant ten-point advantage.

For reasons they'd arbitrarily decided, demerits were awarded for veils (too coy), tie-dye (too obvious) and anything plaid (too Scottish—Mike's assertion being that anyone who wanted to get married in a kilt better be in the Highlands).

By the third day they were replacing what they didn't like with what they did. It started with him saying, "You would look great in one of those shoulderless numbers," when they were watching a woman give her vows while the breeze whipped her sleeveless gown around her so she looked like a Greek statue.

"Board shorts," she'd retaliated.

"Board shorts?"

"I love you in board shorts."

The devil lights were in his eyes. "What's the winning score so far?"

"I think the one where everyone including the minister had bare feet, and her bouquet was made of seaweed and cowrie shells."

"One shell," he'd corrected.

"We don't know that for sure. There could have been others."

Already he was chuckling. "And then at the end she threw them all in the sea."

"And then he took off his necklace of shark's teeth and threw that in the ocean."

She'd snorted. "And then she yelled at him and made him go fish it out."

"So then they all ended up wading into the surf trying to find his necklace, because it was her wedding gift to him."

They'd stood side by side on their balcony overlooking the aqua-blue of the water and the white crescent of sand. The moon was heavy and golden and the breeze carried magic. For all their joking, she'd felt the magic being absorbed into her skin, being breathed into her body. He had turned her to him and kissed her slowly. That man could enjoy a romantic moment with the best of them. Mmm. And he knew how to kiss her until she was boneless with desire.

He broke away slowly, running his hand down her bare back. "Why don't we show them how it's done?"

"How what's done?" she'd murmured, reaching for him again.

He held her off for a moment. "How to get married on a beach."

Her blood seemed to follow the same rhythm as the surf; she heard it pounding in her ears. "Are you saying what I think you're saying?"

"Yeah." He took a quick breath. "Let's get married."

She'd laughed. "What, here?"

"Yes." He looked suddenly young, boyish. "Tomorrow. The next day. Whenever they can fit us in."

He had kissed her then, the kind of kiss that made every thought fly out of her head. "I love you, Taylor."

The truth settled around her, warm and comforting. They'd never said the words, but she knew in that moment they were true. "I love you, too."

"So, we'll do it?"

"But…our families, our friends…what about…" Her head was spinning.

He'd waved her objections away. "Too complicated. My folks are divorced and there will be nothing but trouble with 'I'm not coming if he's coming' stuff. We'll have a big party when we get back."

The idea was so crazy and spontaneous and yet so absolutely right that she closed her eyes, listened to that inner voice that rarely led her astray and said, "Yes."

The next day she was in the gift shop buying a pale blue cotton strapless sundress with a form-fitting top and a flowing skirt. Mike wore board shorts and, naturally, they'd both been barefoot. When he presented her with a bouquet of wildflowers she'd felt a lump rise in her throat. In that moment, her life felt perfect. No fear for the future, no worry about what they were doing. There was no moment but this one.

"Miss?"

"Hmm?" She blinked, coming back to the present with a start.

The clerk said, "What do you think of the ecru?" She held out a lacy off-white number. "Does the dress have to be white?"

"I don't know." She looked at Kendall. "What do you think?"

"I think that one's worth trying on."

Determined to hold her concentration here with Kendall and not go wandering off down memory lane, she obediently followed the woman carrying a cloud of tulle and silk in her arms and stepped into a change room with so much gilt and so many mirrors that it could have passed for an anteroom at Versailles.

"Okay, so which one do you want to try on first?" Taylor whispered.

"The ecru, I think."

"Good choice. It will be fabulous with your coloring."

"Did I tell you that Dylan's meeting us here?"

"Dylan? Isn't it bad luck for the groom to see the bride in her wedding dress before the big day?"

"He won't be seeing me in my wedding dress, he'll be seeing you in it."

Taylor giggled and started pulling off her dress. "This is seriously nuts."

"I know. That's what I love about it." So nuts, in fact,

that the race car driver must have forgotten he was playing pool with Mike. Oh, well. Knowing her ex, he'd soon find some other boys to play with. He'd never gone into a sporting venue he couldn't feel at home in.

"What if Dylan's recognized?"

"It doesn't matter. We're sticking to the script you wrote. Hank is the groom. You're the bride. I imagine Dylan will bring him along, too."

"Well, now that Hank is the golden boy of NASCAR, I'm not sure how invisible he's going to be."

From out front came the low rumble of male voices. "Oh, good," said Kendall. "They're here."

Taylor felt an odd flutter behind her heart as she stared at the image of herself in a true bridal gown in the large mirror in the change room. "I am starting to get a very bad feeling about this."

MIKE WAS GETTING A BAD feeling in his gut. When Dylan had approached him to do him a favor, he'd been fine with it. He owed the man after he'd brought him home in a less-than-pristine condition, made sure he got to bed, and then, even more amazing, had resisted the urge to broadcast the incident to a lot of people in the industry who would appreciate the story.

A man who could keep his mouth shut made a good friend, and Mike wasn't a person who forgot a good turn. So, here he was, feeling as though he'd stepped into one of those mysterious female places where men have no business. Even more uncomfortable, he'd agreed to stand in for Dylan as a fake groom instead of Hank. A couple of years ago he'd have thought this a ripe jest and would have enjoyed the experience immensely, but what no one knew was that he'd been married and he'd failed miserably. Asking him to go into a bride boutique was like asking a reformed alcoholic to drop into the local tavern and pick up a six-pack.

At least Taylor had never put him through this bower of frills.

Dylan looked around as though not sure where to rest his eyes. "There is so much—pouf."

"Yeah. I know."

"Why do they need all this white frilly stuff?"

Mike shrugged. "It's a girl thing."

"And which one is the lucky man?" asked a frightening-looking woman with too-smooth hair and too-white skin.

"That would be him," Dylan said, gesturing to Mike.

The scary woman sent him a smile that reminded him of his fifth-grade teacher when he forgot to do his math homework. "Your bride should be out soon."

"Isn't it bad luck to see the dress before the wedding?"

The woman shrugged elegant shoulders. "Modern manners," she said as though she personally washed her hands of any unhappiness resulting from the pre-mature viewing of the dress.

Mike started to feel hot. All those white poofy things seemed to close in around him, and he imagined that tonight he'd dream he was being smothered by marshmallows, choked by clouds.

When the scary woman floated off to talk to a nervous girl who appeared way too young to be getting married, he leaned over and whispered, "So, who is standing in for—"

He never finished. Kendall came out of a doorway, sent a conspiratorial wink their way and said, "Here she is." And out walked Taylor in an honest-to-God, bona fide white wedding dress.

It wasn't all poofy like most of the stuff in here, or so white the dress looked like it had been stored in Crest White Strips. It was a kind of soft, creamy color. Simple and elegant. He was used to seeing Taylor in jeans and sportswear; she rarely wore fancy clothes.

She gave a tiny gasp when their gazes met.

He felt as if he'd taken a nine-iron to the gut.

She blinked, her eyes huge, and he took a step forward. He'd always thought she was hot, and he still remembered the way he'd felt when they got married on that beach in Hawaii, the way the breeze molded her cotton sundress to her body. The way they'd had their own private joke even as they took serious vows.

And here she was, looking like a bride in a magazine. It was as if he was glimpsing something he'd been missing for a long time. In a second it was over. She said, "I thought I was marrying Hank."

Oh, and didn't that just figure.

"He delegated the job to me," Mike said.

Her bridal glow dimmed. "Oh, goodie. My lucky day."

"In your dreams."

"Uh, kids, can we kiss and make up?" Dylan said in a low voice. Mike became aware that the dragon lady had abandoned her teenage prey and was standing near them looking from Mike to Taylor with a puzzled expression on her face.

Okay, he thought, if it wasn't for Dylan he'd be on the street right now headed for the nearest sports bar. Somewhere, on some network, there was a game. Any kind of game. He really didn't care. Something with rules he understood that he could watch for a couple of hours in the company of like-minded individuals. And where no one would be wearing a white gown. But he'd agreed to stand in for Dylan and he wasn't a man to back out on his word.

Taylor pulled herself together faster than he could. She smiled. "Sorry," she said. "We have a tempestuous relationship."

Oh, if she wanted tempests, he could happily provide a few. "That's right," he said, never taking his eyes off his ex-wife. "It's all the passion between us."

She blushed adorably and he felt marginally better.

"What do you think of the dress, Mike?" Dylan said, giving him a sharp elbow in the ribs, reminding him of why they were there.

"I'm not too sure, Dy. What do you think of the dress?" he parroted back.

Dylan glanced at Kendall, who made a kind of a wishy-washy gesture with her hands.

Well, hell, he thought. If he was being asked to stand in for a lovesick groom he had a right to act like one.

"I don't know about them, honey," he said, "but I have never seen you look more beautiful."

She tried to glare at him without anyone else knowing, but he had nothing to lose and somehow he felt he'd been led astray here. Nobody'd told him he'd be required to make a fool of himself in the name of friendship. He figured there ought to be some kind of compensation, so he walked up, about as starry eyed as he imagined a groom would be if he was fool enough to voluntarily enter the House of Lace, and while the rest of them looked on, dumbfounded, he kissed Taylor full on the lips.

It was more of a peck than anything, but he liked the way she felt in his arms, loved the familiar flavor of her on his lips, and the half protest, half sigh as they fell into each other once more. He'd forgotten how powerful their connection was. How had they ever been crazy enough to let this go?

For a moment after he raised his head she stood there, staring at him with her eyes wide and vulnerable. Then her lips clamped shut and she turned heel and strode back into the change room, the swirl of dress following her in an angry swish.

Kendall, with one furious glare his way, stalked after her.

When the dragon lady moved to help another sucker who'd entered her store, Dylan said in a fierce undertone, "What are you doing?"

"You want me to act like a groom? I'm acting like a groom."

"Well, don't do it again."

It took all Mike's self-control not to tell Dylan exactly why he would do it again. And soon.

"I AM SO SORRY," KENDALL said the minute she and Taylor were back in the gilt-and-mirrored change room. "I can't believe Mike did that."

"No biggie," Taylor insisted, busying herself with trying to get herself out of the dress and mortified that she'd felt the old rush of desire the second Mike had touched her. Had she learned nothing? "But I thought Hank was standing in."

"So did I, but I guess he figured he was too high · profile now he did so well in Daytona and all, so maybe he suggested that Dylan give Mike a call."

Taylor stopped midzipper, the dress half-on and half-off. "Hank suggested Mike Lundquist?"

"I think so."

"That man has a seriously disturbed sense of humor."

"I didn't know you and Mike didn't get along."

"It's complicated," she wailed, wishing, not for the first time, that she was back on a dive boat headed for the Great Barrier Reef, where her most complicated decision in a day was scuba or snorkel?

"Look, you don't have to do this if you don't want to," Kendall said, looking abashed.

"No. I want to help, of course I do. This will be fun. Really." She was a team player, she reminded herself. She could do this. "So, what did you think of this one?"

"I'm not sure. I kind of fell in love with that gown I saw in the magazine."

"Well, we have more choices," she said, gesturing to the gowns still hanging.

She modeled four more gowns, refusing to let Mike get to her as she walked out in one bridal gown after another.

He also behaved, and there was no more inappropriate kissing. He stuck to sardonic comments and jokes.

"What do you think of that one, Mike?" Dylan asked when she tottered out in a gown with so many frills she felt like Scarlett O'Hara before the war.

Mike studied her with a hand on his chin as though she were a rare painting he was thinking of buying. "Turn around," he ordered.

She did, letting the skirt bell around her.

Mike shook his head. "My great-aunt Mildred used to crochet dresses for dolls exactly like that. She gave them away as toilet-roll covers."

And they'd had one, she recalled. Mike had, of course, named the doll Lulu and hung a sign around her neck that said, "Well, I never…"

At the end of an hour she was sick of squeezing into bridal gowns and Kendall didn't look as though she'd fallen in love with any of them. Taylor thought nothing had looked as good as that first gown, but she wasn't going to say a word. It wasn't her wedding. Thank goodness.

When they left the store, Kendall confirmed what Taylor had already guessed. "I didn't fall in love with any of them. Did you, Dylan?"

He walked along, holding hands comfortably with his fiancée while Mike and Taylor followed behind, walking a good foot apart from each other. "I thought the first dress looked great on Taylor, but I don't think it would be right for you."

"I thought the very same thing," said Kendall, turning to beam at Taylor. "If you ever get married, you'll have to remember that dress."

She didn't dare turn her head to glance at Mike. She didn't have to; she could feel him beside her and all the history between them as thick as humidity.

"I'll keep that in mind," she promised.

"Sorry it didn't work out," Mike said, clearly feeling as uncomfortable as she did that they'd fallen into two couples. "But I really have to get going. I've got a story to file."

"But we have more bridal boutiques to visit," Kendall said, flashing her list.

"Look," Dylan said, "why don't you women narrow down the choices and Mike and I will help with the final selection?"

"Oh. Okay. I guess."

"We'll have fun, just us girls," Taylor agreed, only too glad to lose the male company that was giving her a headache.

"Okay. Thank you for being a good sport," Kendall said. "Same time next week?"

If Taylor hadn't been as horrified as her ex-husband she'd have laughed at his expression. "Next week?"

"Well, I still need a dress. By next week we should be down to the finals."

CHAPTER THIRTEEN

HANK WAS DETERMINED TO repeat his glorious performance in California the next week, but perhaps the most interesting development, from Taylor's point of view, was his choice of companion for the race.

When she asked him if he wanted her to make arrangements for his date, he said, "Nah. It's okay. I've got it under control."

Thinking he simply hadn't met anyone suitable, or that Denise and Cutie Pie had put him off models temporarily, she didn't push the matter.

So she was more than a little surprised to see Louise Hunnicut, the biking champ, at his motor home Friday. She and Hank wore biking clothes and both were still glowing from what she guessed was a long ride. The two were obviously still hitting it off, and she thought the chances were good they were going to move from friends to something warmer.

Incredibly, she felt bad for Mike. Losing a woman he liked to a NASCAR driver had to be a blow. After greeting the young woman she said, "Does Mike know you're here?"

Louise glanced at her with a blank expression and then said, "Oh, you mean that reporter?"

"Yes. The one you were with when I met you?"

"Right. He was writing a profile about me. Now I think he wants to include me in a feature he's doing about Hank and the women in his life." She gasped, her gaze flying to Hank's. "Not that I meant—" She looked at Taylor, who watched her blush the blush of a redhead. "Hank and I are just friends."

"For now," Hank said, looking equally conscious.

Figuring this was a perfect moment to make an exit, Taylor excused herself on some pretext and found herself grinning as she walked away from Hank's motor home.

What a cute couple they made.

And Mike had never been interested in her as anything but a story.

Taylor enjoyed her second race, with Hank finishing a respectable twelfth. She had bumped into Mike a few times and was able to be friendly even when he made low-voiced comments about her new occupation as a wedding-dress model.

Back in the office Monday, she was sending out her report to the sponsors when Reena walked in with a copy of the newspaper. "Did you see this?"

"See what? Did Hank get more coverage?"

The woman beamed at her. "Not only Hank. You did, too. And there's a picture."

"There is?" She snatched at the paper. Sure enough, there was a photo of her and Hank taken at

Daytona at the end of the race. He'd picked her right up off the ground and swung her around. They were both laughing and you could see the bond between them. It was a good photograph, she thought, in that it told a story.

So did Mike's copy.

Behind every great NASCAR driver is a woman. It can be a wife, girlfriend, mother or, in Hank Mission's case, a public relations manager.

Maybe it's too early to say that rookie driver Mission is great, but his second-place finish at Daytona suggests he's going to be a driver to watch. Even his twelfth-place finish this past weekend was impressive.

Mission is quick to credit his team for his amazing success so far, including rookie PR manager, Taylor Robinson. "Taylor's like a big sister in a lot of ways. She doesn't take any crap. She's also really well organized and keeps me focused. She's an important part of my team..."

The article went on to talk about Hank's mother and grandmother and briefly mentioned fellow athlete and North Carolinian, Louise Hunnicut, as a fan and new friend. There was a photo of the two of them in California before the race looking a whole lot better together, in Taylor's opinion, than Hank and the swimsuit model.

When she finished reading, she put the paper down and glanced up to find Reena looking awfully pleased with herself. "Mike wrote that article for you, honey."

"He did not," she scoffed. "He wanted to find a fresh way to write a feature about a rookie driver, that's all."

Her old friend hoisted a hip onto Taylor's desk, already a lot messier than when she'd started. "You accused me of deliberately bringing you two together. You thought I was matchmaking."

"Weren't you?"

"Maybe. The thing is, my kids are all married and happy. I've got grandchildren. Honey, you know I look on you like another daughter, especially now your dad's gone. Frankly, if one of my kids was acting the way you and Mike are, I'd lay down the law and force them into counseling."

Taylor knew she wasn't kidding and was momentarily glad Reena wasn't her mom.

"You know what happened."

"I do. You had an awful time. Your dad got sick, you lost the baby, and Mike and you, instead of supporting each other when times got tough, fell apart. But you still love each other, I can see it."

"When have you seen us together?"

"When you came storming in after him in nothing but a sweaty running shirt and skimpy shorts."

"Oh," she said, remembering the day well.

"He couldn't follow you into your office fast enough."

"Doesn't mean he loves me."

"Taylor, when are you going to stop with the punishment?" Reena demanded.

"I'm not punishing Mike for what happened."

The older woman shook her head, looking sad. "Not Mike, you."

TAYLOR STOOD LOOKING OUT her window down into the dim courtyard, letting the sweat of her run dry on her body while she sipped water. She could hear the singing hum of crickets out there. The outdoor lamps cast glimmering silver dollars onto the green space below her apartment window.

Her run hadn't helped at all. She still felt a sort of ache behind her diaphragm. Longing, that's what it was, gut-deep yearning for the man she loved to the bottom of her being. The man she'd pushed away.

Was it possible Reena was right? Was she punishing herself for what had happened?

Something inside her had broken apart, she realized, during that awful time when her father died and she lost the baby.

She did feel guilt, she realized. Deep down she believed that if she hadn't caused the miscarriage, her actions had certainly contributed. Mike had begged her to stay put, saying there was nothing she could do for her father. He was in a coma. But she hadn't listened. She'd flown down to sit at his bedside, pushed herself to exhaustion sitting there almost around the clock for the better part of a week.

He died without ever regaining consciousness.

After she lost the baby, she hadn't grieved delicately. She'd ranted and yelled at Mike. Maybe he'd been awfully quick to take refuge in work and sports, but she knew she'd pushed him away.

Reena was right. She could never move on until she came to terms with what had happened between Mike and her.

When he'd stared at her in that wedding dress everything had come rushing back. All the feelings she'd once had for him, and she thought she'd seen his for her reflected back at her.

She looked out across the courtyard of her apartment complex. On the other side, through the windows that faced hers, she saw a couple, obviously also fresh home from work. They were chatting, the way couples do at the end of the day, and from here she could almost imagine the conversation. "How did that presentation go? Did you hire a new assistant? If I brown the chicken, can you make the salad?" The simple routines and everyday pleasures of being a couple.

Unconsciously, she placed a protective hand across her belly.

The ache behind her diaphragm grew worse and her breathing more ragged than when she'd first arrived home after her run. She was so lonely. She hadn't felt lonely when she was traveling Australia by herself, or maybe she simply hadn't allowed herself to feel it. But now she did. Because she'd had that relationship she was watching across the courtyard, the easy familiarity, the comfort of friendship and the passion of lovers. She'd had it with Mike, and then, the second things had become difficult, she'd run. Fast and far.

Now they were in the same city, connected once more by work, and she felt so lonely for him that she ached.

She looked at the phone. What if she called him? What if she broke their unwritten rule and called him and invited him over for dinner? An image of the way he'd looked at her when she'd been wearing that wedding dress flashed across her mind again. The way he'd kissed her as though he still had the right.

She picked up the phone, then realized she didn't even know his number. She'd have to get it from information. She imagined the phone conversation once she got hold of him. How would she even start off? What would she say? What if some woman answered his phone, or he refused her invitation?

No, worst of all, what if he accepted?

Never in her life had she felt more confused. Not only did she not *know* her own mind, she pretty much thought she was out of it entirely.

She put the cordless back into its cradle and walked into the bathroom. She showered, rubbed moisturizer into her skin, threw on some clean jeans and a T-shirt and settled in front of the TV with a single-girl dinner of salad and sparkling water.

She was tired, she reminded herself. She'd been working like a maniac learning her job, doing her job and trying to keep up with Hank and his amazing career. Definitely, she could use a night off. Trouble was, all the mindless tasks like cleaning and laundry left her mind free to contemplate the mess she had made of things, and the unresolved issues in her life.

One of which was how she felt about her ex-husband.

When she settled into bed that night, she felt him beside her, an unseen presence. She felt his arm around her, the way they used to settle to sleep, felt it so strongly that she imagined if she spoke to him he might answer her.

Of course, she didn't dare test her theory because she couldn't bear the silence when he didn't reply.

THE PHONE WAS RINGING. When Taylor was in the office, typically Monday to Wednesday, it seemed the phone was always ringing.

Hank was suddenly somebody, which meant her job was becoming both more exciting and more demanding each day. Taylor had never had so much fun.

She picked up. "Taylor Robinson."

"Hey, Taylor. Mike here."

He'd never called her. Not since they broke up. There was a short pause before she said, "Hi," and waited.

"Look, I need a favor," he said.

"Okay. What is it?"

"We're doing this series of Day in a Life features. My editor wants me to do one on Hank."

"Sounds interesting," she said, knowing already

that Hank's schedule was as full as it could hold. But he'd done a nice job on the profile and she wanted to help him out.

"I know. He's hot and everybody wants a piece of him, but we've had so much positive feedback on the profile that he asked me to give it a shot."

"It was a really nice feature," she said. "You did a good job."

"Glad you liked it." He sounded genuinely pleased.

"What do you need?"

"A day. I basically tail him and talk to him for a bit."

"What kind of timing are you looking at?"

"A race day would be my preference, sometime in the next three to four weeks."

"I'll talk to Hank. Let me see what I can do."

"Thanks."

There was a pause. He didn't hang up and neither did she.

"So," he finally said, "how's it going?"

She settled back in her chair, glanced around the office at the stacks of magazines and the new poster of Hank framed on her wall, at the computer screen open to her driver's calendar. "It's going well," she said.

"Like the new job?"

"More than I thought I would."

"Do you miss journalism?"

Was he criticizing? Somehow, she didn't think so, he sounded like he really wanted to know.

"Not really. I'm having too much fun with what I'm doing. Learning new skills and all."

"You're good at the job," he said, sounding sincere.

She felt a smile bloom. Crazy that it should matter what her ex-husband thought of her abilities in her new job, but it did. "Thanks. It's been quite the learning curve, but I'm starting to feel like I fit in."

"Watching races live at the track is better than when we used to watch them on big-screen TV, back in Seattle," he said.

She thought back on how they'd first become friends and then fallen in love in the glow of those big screens. "That was pretty fun, too," she said softly.

"Yeah. It was."

There was another pause. "Do you think we could—"

"Damn it, editorial meeting's started. I've got to go." And before she could say goodbye, he was gone. Without letting her finish her sentence.

She supposed he'd given her her answer. The response to "Do you think we could—" was clearly and unequivocally no. She wasn't even certain herself how she would have ended that sentence. It was half out before her brain had caught up with her mouth. She thought she was going to say, "Do you think we could be friends?"

That was what she missed most, she thought, Mike's friendship. Nobody ever got her the way he did or made her laugh the way he could.

Oh, well. Trying to be friends was probably a stupid idea, anyway.

She went back to her computer, looking at how she could fit Mike into Hank's crowded schedule. She did love her job. After leaving Seattle and a promising career in such a hurry it was good to be working again, proving herself once more. Did she miss journalism?

She thought about it. Her goal had always been to work for a while and then, when she had kids, she'd imagined working as a freelance journalist so she could stay home with her babies. She was taking a break for a different reason than she'd imagined, but it wasn't a big deal not to be writing now. She'd pick it up again at some point in her life.

Mike had been completely supportive of her decision to work from home, she remembered. For a second she closed her eyes against a wave of regret. If things had worked out differently…

But they hadn't.

She typed a note into Hank's calendar slotting Mike in. She used green text, which meant Unconfirmed. There were plenty of notations in black, which meant they were confirmed, and even more in green, the tentative ones. She and Hank would work together to decide which events, appearances and media opportunities he'd commit to.

She was getting ready to send him the latest version of his calendar for the week when Hank strolled all the way into her office instead of hovering in the doorway like he usually did.

"How's it going?" he asked her.

"You're keeping me busy."

He grinned. "Excellent. And then you keep me busy."

"Seems to be the way it works."

"I need to take a quick trip home. My grandmother's sick. Can I blow off tomorrow and Wednesday?"

"Of course, if it's a family emergency."

"It's not that bad. She broke her arm a couple of months ago and she just got the cast off." He shrugged. "She's miserable because her arm is still weak. My mom thought that if I went home for a visit it would cheer her up."

"Okay." She looked over his schedule. "Yeah, there's nothing here that can't be rescheduled. I'll get right on it."

"Thanks, Taylor. You take the time off too. You've been working too hard."

"Oh, well, I'm shopping with Kendall tomorrow morning, but I've got lots to keep me busy in the afternoon."

"No. I mean it. I really want you to take the time off. I want you extra fresh this weekend—" he leaned toward her and dropped his voice "—because I am planning to win."

She laughed. "Thanks for the warning, but you know what? I always think you're going to win."

"That's why we make such a great team. We both think I'm fabulous."

It was the twinkle in his eyes, she decided, that

let him get away with his outrageous behavior. "I'll make sure to put that in your media messages."

He walked around and looked over her shoulder at his schedule. "What's this?"

"Mike Lundquist just called. He wants to profile you for a Day in the Life feature in his paper."

"Cool. When?"

She raised her brows in surprise. "Are you sure you want to? It's a whole day of being followed around by a reporter. Which means being on your best behavior."

"Sure. I can do it. Besides, he'll write a flattering profile of me."

"What makes you so sure of that?"

He sent her that devilish expression. "He stole my bride. He owes me a favor."

"And speaking of that," she said. "Thanks for passing me on. I feel like a toaster that got regifted."

He laughed. "He's a good guy, a friend of Dy's, and he sure seems to like you. I should have told you I was bailing but I kind of got busy."

"Well, I hope your grandmother makes you play three thousand hands of gin rummy, because I am stuck wedding-dress shopping tomorrow. Again."

"Yeah, I'm real sorry to miss that," he said.

She grabbed an elastic band out of the tray where she kept them, getting a bull's-eye on his back. There was something satisfying about surprising someone with an elastic-band missile.

"No," he said, laughing. "Really, I'm sorry." And

then he showed the great good sense to head out of her office as fast as his long legs would carry him, so he was gone before her next missile launched.

CHAPTER FOURTEEN

TUESDAY DAWNED. ANOTHER bridal shopping day. This time, Taylor was determined Kendall would go home with a dress. How hard could it be? If she'd been able to buy a wedding dress in ten minutes in a hotel-lobby store, she thought two full days in bridal boutiques should yield Kendall's gown.

When the phone rang and it was Kendall on the other end, she hoped the woman was calling to cancel. A day at home to putter around, do some washing and mundane chores, maybe even water her ficus, would be heaven. But no, it seemed Kendall wasn't calling to cancel. She'd moved up the meeting time. And she sounded excited. "Listen, can you be ready by ten?"

"Um, yes, sure."

"Great, we'll pick you up on our way downtown. Oh, and can you pack a change of clothes for somewhere nice for dinner? Dy wants to take us out as a way of saying thanks to you and Mike for your help."

"It's fine, really. No thanks necessary."

"You don't have plans for tonight, do you?" Kendall sounded ridiculously disappointed.

"No. I don't have plans. I just don't want you feeling you have to take me for dinner." And in the company of her ex, who had made it clear he didn't want to be friends with her.

"Trust me, we'll have fun," Kendall said.

No doubt Kendall would, Taylor thought sourly as she threw her only little black dress into a bag with black heels, a change of underwear and her makeup kit.

Dylan and Kendall arrived five minutes early looking disgustingly pleased with themselves and far too in love.

Once they had Taylor's bag thrown in the back and were on their way, Kendall immediately started discussing bridesmaids' dresses. Taylor made polite noises to indicate that she was listening when really she was wondering how soon she could have Kendall in a dress she liked, with venue, flowers and anything else that needed booking booked and be done with all of this subterfuge.

"So, I was thinking teal-blue would be nice, but if you prefer the dusky rose, I'm fine with that, too."

She realized the woman was looking at her with brows raised, waiting for an answer. "I think you should decide. It's your wedding."

"But you'll be wearing the dress."

The truth struck her like a thunderbolt. "Me? You want me to be a bridesmaid?"

"Maid of honor, actually. I can't think of anyone better. I know we haven't known each other long, but

I feel like we're friends, and this whole wedding-planning experience is such a bonding time. So, what do you say? Will you do it?"

What could she say? She ought to be a matron of honor, but she wasn't going there. "Well, of course. I'd love to. Thanks."

"You're my only attendant. With your coloring I think teal, don't you?"

"Teal is fine."

"Excellent. See? You're the perfect maid of honor already."

"Where are we going?" Taylor asked as the car headed away from the shopping areas of town.

"We're picking Mike up."

Her stomach dipped. She and Mike stuck in the backseat together. That should be fun.

He seemed to share her enthusiasm for backseat sharing and wedding-dress shopping based on the way he rolled his eyes as he got in so only she could see him.

He'd thrown an overnighter bag in the back as well, so now she knew he hadn't had any plans tonight, either. Not that she should care if he had company on a Tuesday night or not.

Kendall turned around once the car was moving again. There was an air of suppressed excitement about her. "So, we have a surprise," she said.

"Oh, goodie," Mike said under his breath.

Taylor choked back a laugh and said, "What is it?"

"How would you like to go to New York?"

"When?"

"Right now."

"Uh—"

"My heart's set on that dress I saw in the magazine. It's in New York."

Taylor nodded, remembering the dress and agreeing with her friend that it would look fabulous on her.

"Maybe you could have it shipped."

"Better idea. Dylan's chartered a plane. We'll be in the Big Apple before you know it."

"You're going to fly to New York City to try on a dress?" Mike asked in a tone of disbelief.

"Why not?" Taylor said, jumping to her friend's defense. "You guys fly all over the country to drive cars too fast." She narrowed her gaze on Mike. "Or to write about guys who drive too fast."

"Ouch," he said, miming a wound to the chest.

"I'm simply saying that one is no more silly than the other."

"Dy, what is the appropriate response to that?"

"Dignified silence, buddy. Stick with dignified silence."

"Well, have a good time. You won't need me and Taylor."

"Yes, we do," Dylan said.

"Oh, please say you'll come. We've got it all organized. We'll have so much fun. We're picking up my ring at Tiffany's. We have to celebrate. We'll be back tomorrow, anytime you say."

Now she realized why Hank had been so adamant she should take a couple of days off. Once more, there'd been some backroom dealing between him and Dylan.

"Well, um..." Taylor glanced at Mike, who was looking at her oddly.

"Fine by me," he said. "I like New York."

What could she say? She liked New York, too, she just wasn't sure she wanted to see it with her ex. However, if there was any hope of them becoming friends again, this was a good opportunity to try it out. "Sure. It will be fun."

She was becoming used to flying on private planes by now, but it was still a thrill. She and Kendall went over Kendall's super-organized wedding-planning to-do list. Since Kendall didn't trust a wedding planner to keep her secret, she'd decided to do the job herself. No one could have been more organized in Taylor's opinion.

The guys talked sports.

They landed at La Guardia just after noon and there was a town car and driver waiting. Being a rich NASCAR driver certainly had its advantages, she thought, as she slid into the backseat.

Their first stop was an exclusive bridal shop. As they drew up, Kendall patted her stomach. "I'm nervous. What if we've come all this way and I hate the dress?"

"You'll find something fabulous, I know it," Taylor said.

"Excellent encouragement. You're the best maid of honor I ever had."

"Thanks."

They walked up four steps to get to the door, and before they opened it, Kendall said, "Call me superstitious, but I'm not lying to anyone this time. I'm the bride, damn it. I'm trying on my own dress, and if your mother finds out about the wedding…" She petered out and looked at Dylan who merely raised his brows. "Well, we'll think of something."

"Celine is still in Vegas, I think. I doubt she can sing at your wedding."

"Madonna might be free," Dylan murmured.

"I have a connection in Nashville," Mike offered. "I might have a line on Emmylou Harris."

"Would you guys stop?" Kendall said, half laughing. "I don't want any household names at my wedding except Dylan and his NASCAR buddies." She took a deep breath. "And if I have to tell your mother to butt out, Dy, I will."

"I knew there was a reason I fell in love with you," Dylan said, taking her hand and kissing it.

The four of them walked in and a young, pretty woman wearing a sleek navy dress and pearls approached them. "Hi. Which one's the bride?"

"I am," Kendall said, and she sounded so happy that Taylor wanted to hug her. It was easy to get cynical about love and marriage, but when you saw two people who worked so well together, how could you help but believe in happily ever after?

"Do you have anything particular in mind?" the woman asked, leading them deeper into bridal heaven. Vera Wang, Givenchy, Chanel… If they'd ever designed a bridal gown, they were represented. Her heels sank into the rich carpeting as they followed the woman. There was a slight floral scent in the air.

"Yes," said Kendall, pulling a folded magazine page from her bag and showing it to the young woman.

"Oh, fabulous choice for you. Simple, clean lines, absolute elegance."

It was the only gown she tried on. The second the tiny buttons were done up and she turned to face the mirror, Taylor knew Kendall had found her perfect dress.

"It was made for you, Kendall," she said, feeling unaccountably misty. "You look so beautiful."

They both stared at Kendall's reflection in the mirror while the saleswoman put a few pins here and there and pronounced it perfect. "We can have this dress ready in three weeks."

"I can't believe it. This is the perfect dress." She turned slowly around. "It's not that there weren't great dresses in those other stores, but I'd already seen the dress I wanted."

"I know. Are you going to show Dylan?" Taylor asked.

She bit her lip. "No. I think I must be more superstitious than I thought. What if he sees me in the dress before our wedding and then we end up getting divorced one day? I don't want the guilt of thinking it was because I showed off my dress too soon."

The young salesclerk agreed. "No one should see your dress before the wedding but you and your bridesmaids. And maybe a few special female relatives."

"And speaking of bridesmaids, my maid of honor here needs a dress."

The bridesmaid dress they chose was the least bridesmaidy dress Taylor had ever seen. It wasn't teal, but a pale green cocktail-length, pretty and feminine. She loved it.

"Thank you for not making me look like a fruit."

"A what?"

"Haven't you ever noticed that most bridesmaids' dresses are colors like apricot, cherry, peach or some kind of melon?"

Kendall laughed. "This is more of a mint." Then she impulsively hugged Taylor. "We're going to look fabulous."

"Yes, we are." After the marathon day when they'd ended up with nothing, Taylor was beyond relieved to have so much progress completed in such a short time. "I can't believe that was so easy."

"I know. Now we need to get a few more things and we're done."

The few more things included a tux for Dylan, fortunately in an equally fancy shop next door, ordering wedding invitations from the fanciest stationer Taylor had ever seen, and then Tiffany's.

"Listen, Dy," Mike said when they got to the familiar landmark on Fifth Avenue, "Taylor and I will do some window-shopping while you get your ring."

Taylor gave him full marks for tact even as she dreaded being alone with him. Still, she could always ditch him. Who needed a man when Fifth Avenue stretched ahead like the road to paradise?

"Taylor?" Kendall asked, a concerned look on her face. "Are you sure you don't want to come with us?"

"You two should pick out the ring together." Then she held out her arms as the glorious truth struck her. "I'm on Fifth Avenue and I have a credit card," she said with a grin. "Go ahead and dump me."

"Okay." They agreed to meet at their hotel, a top-rated boutique hotel in Midtown, in two hours. Taylor and Mike watched as the bride and groom headed into Tiffany's hand in hand.

"That was a nice thing you did," Taylor said.

"I figured they wanted to be alone. Besides, I do not want to be called on to give advice on princess cut versus bezel."

She laughed. "Lucky for you there wasn't much selection in the gift shop in Hawaii." She could have bitten off her tongue for bringing up their wedding, but he merely laughed.

"That pink coral ring looked damned good on you."

"I always liked it," she said, feeling nostalgia

creep up on her along with the smell of hot dogs from a street vendor.

"You still have it?"

"Somewhere."

There was silence for a second as they stood there looking at each other. Then she shook off the unfamiliar mood. "Well, I don't know about you, but I am going shopping."

"I think I've had about all the shopping I can stand for one day. I'll go for a walk. See what I find."

She nodded, relieved that he had no intention of following her.

"I'll meet you back at the hotel."

"Can you find it okay?"

"I'll manage."

He headed one way while she went the other.

By the time she grabbed a cab, almost two hours later, she was nicely laden with bags and her feet hurt. An excellent afternoon's shopping.

Her room at the hotel was sleek, modern and utterly luxurious. There was a message on her room phone that they were meeting in the lobby at seven for a drink. She squeaked when she realized it was after six and threw herself into the shower. She spent some time on her hair and on applying some of the new makeup she'd bought today, used her new toothbrush and then slid into the new lingerie, and the much nicer little black dress that she'd been unable to resist.

When she got to the lobby at a few minutes before

seven, Kendall and Dylan were already there. The glow of happiness in Kendall's eyes made her own light up. "Well? Did you get it?"

She held out her left hand and Taylor oohed and aahed at the emerald-cut diamond solitaire, which was large enough to draw attention but not ostentatious. "It's gorgeous," she said.

"Thanks."

She handed Taylor an iconic blue box. "We got you a bridesmaid present."

"Ohmygod. You shouldn't have."

She opened the box and there were a pair of dainty diamond drop earrings. "Oh, oh, oh, I love them."

She stood there in the lobby and attempted to jab the earrings into her lobes.

She hadn't heard Mike arrive, but suddenly he was there. "You are so impatient," he said, taking the earring out of her hand and raising her chin. "Hold still," he said.

How many times had they done things like this? She doubted he even realized how much he was revealing. His fingers felt warm and familiar against her chin, and while he focused on her lobe, she had the leisure to study his face up close. He'd just shaved, she realized, seeing the smoothness of his skin. Only a hint of shadow indicated where he'd sport stubble in a few hours. His eyes were espresso dark, his hair black and tumbling over his forehead the way it always did.

He smelled the same. She wanted to close her eyes and breathe him in.

She felt her chest rising and falling with her breath, felt her own hair shifting against her neck as he pushed it behind her ears to fit the second earring in her ear.

"All done," he said with a quick smile. He leaned forward and for a second she thought he was going to kiss her, as he would have done if they had really traveled back in time the way this felt.

But he caught himself in time and gave her a quick pat on the shoulder before turning to say something to Dylan about women and their jewelry.

The dinner was a huge success. Dylan and Kendall were happy, Mike was funny, and she'd always been his best audience. At least, that's what he used to tell her. She and Mike were soon as festive as the happy couple.

The town car dropped them off back at the hotel. Dylan and Kendall were clearly in a hurry to say good-night.

Taylor and Mike looked at each other. "You two go ahead," Mike said. "I want to show Taylor the spot where Joe DiMaggio married Marilyn Monroe."

"Great. See you in the morning," said Dylan, practically dragging Kendall into the elevator.

"How did Joe DiMaggio marry Marilyn Monroe in a hotel that wasn't built yet?"

"I couldn't think of anything except that there was no way I was getting in that elevator with those two."

"Good thing they don't know that the wedding also took place in San Francisco."

"I could have said I was showing you the place where martians abducted me when I was a kid and they'd have said, 'Fine, okay, good night.'"

She chuckled. "I wouldn't take that bet. Do you think it's safe to get another elevator?"

"Sure, unless you want to take a walk with me. Explore Manhattan by night."

Did she? It was getting too weird being with him all the time and surrounded by wedding fever. The entire experience was bringing back too many memories, some good, some bad, but the combination was pushing her off balance.

She shook her head. "It's been a hectic day. I think I'll turn in."

If he was disappointed, he hid it well. "Pleasant dreams," he said, and turned to the street door.

CHAPTER FIFTEEN

KENDALL AND DYLAN'S WEDDING day dawned exactly as sunny and perfect as every wedding day should. The July sun shone, but not too hot, and a light breeze licked the flowers in the garden of Gordon Winfield's house on Lake Norman where the two would exchange their vows. Since Kendall and Dylan had also bought a house on Lake Norman, they would soon be neighbors.

Taylor couldn't believe the big day had finally arrived. There'd been almost a dozen races between the time she'd come up with the crazy wedding-decoy idea and now. Races that were starting to blur together in her memory. Hotel rooms that she couldn't tell apart.

Since she'd turned down his offer of a walk in Manhattan the night they'd shopped in New York, she and Mike had lapsed into a friendly enough relationship that was all business. They bumped into each other in the garage area and the pits. They'd say "hi" or simply wave. If her heart always lurched in a very unbusinesslike way, she figured that was her problem. She'd get over it in time.

In her down times there'd been wedding prepara-
tions—this maid of honor business was a serious
undertaking, she'd discovered. Especially since
Kendall was frighteningly well organized and left
nothing to chance.

However, once she'd made the decision in New
York not to hide her wedding anymore, Taylor had
seen a new woman emerge. She had loved the story
of how Kendall had insisted Dylan take her down to
visit his parents. On that visit, she'd showed off her
new engagement ring and laid down the law. Taylor
hadn't heard all the details of that memorable con-
frontation, but, looking around at the gorgeous
grounds, she knew Kendall had got her way. Not a
president, ex-president, congressman or a singer
who'd appeared in Vegas or won a Grammy was
present.

In fact, there was a casual atmosphere that no one
knew better than Taylor had taken a huge amount of
work to create.

The tents were perfectly positioned, so they
appeared casually dropped on the lawn by giant
hands. Waiters in Dylan's racing colors instead of
stuffy tuxes would wander among the guests, dis-
pensing drinks and appetizers as soon as the
ceremony was over. A quartet played in front of the
rose arbor.

Kendall had her wish, Taylor thought. The garden
wedding at home was casual, but everything was
first class.

She peeked out of the upper windows of the Winfield home and watched the guests take their seats in the garden. Kendall's mother had arrived earlier, an older version of Kendall and one, Taylor was amused to note, who'd obviously passed on the organizing gene.

"I think pinning the flower headpiece slightly to the left will look better in photographs," she said, her nimble fingers busy. Kendall and Taylor exchanged one helpless glance in the mirror, and then Taylor turned away to busy herself with unbuttoning the dress, readying it for Kendall to step into.

"Take my advice, Taylor. When you get married, elope," Kendall said, dusting her nose with powder at her mother's direction.

Taylor would never have a mother to fuss over her, of course, but she'd have Reena, who would do an admirable job standing in. She shook her head.

"I'm going to have a wedding like this one. Traditional. There's something about eloping that's too much like running away." And she was beginning to think she'd done enough running in her time.

"Can I plan your wedding?" Kendall asked. "I'm an excellent wedding planner. I think I have a real talent for this."

Taylor laughed. "Excellent. I have my wedding planner all picked out. Now all I need is a groom."

"What about—"

"Darling, the time," Kendall's mother said, glancing at the clock on the dresser.

"Oh, right. Better not be late for my own wedding."

When Kendall and her mother had decided the hair and makeup were flawless, Taylor helped her bride into her dress.

As she did up the tiny buttons and the three women chatted and giggled, she decided that if she ever got married again she was definitely going to have this. A traditional wedding, with women helping her on with her clothes.

A wedding was a ceremony. It should be celebrated by a person's friends and community. A backyard post-nuptial party simply didn't do the job.

Taylor's cell phone rang. This was their cue.

"Hello?"

"How's the bride holding up?" Mike asked.

"Fantastic. How's the groom?"

"Looks pretty green around the gills. I think the Scotch for breakfast helped."

She glanced out the window. She could see from here that Dylan was gazing up at the window, eagerness in every line of his body. All the guests were seated.

"How can you tease at a time like this?" She shook her head reprovingly even though he couldn't see her. "We're on our way."

She put down her phone and turned. Kendall glowed with happiness, giving her a quiet beauty.

"Ready?"

She nodded.

On impulse, the three women hugged—gently—and Kendall's mother touched her daughter's cheek before the three of them headed downstairs.

"Shoulders back, girls. Big smiles. This is a happy day."

Yes it was, thought Taylor as she stepped out of the French doors and began the short walk up the grassy aisle. The string quartet moved smoothly into Mozart. Behind her, Kendall had chosen to walk up the aisle on her widowed mother's arm.

Dylan was gazing in goofy-eyed adoration at the woman who looked stunning in the simple gown she'd flown to New York to pick up.

However, his best man's gaze was glued to Taylor.

She couldn't help returning his stare as she walked slowly up the aisle. He was gorgeous in a tux. How had she never known he could dress up so well?

When she reached the top he leaned over and said, "You look beautiful."

"Thanks," she whispered back. "I can't believe we made it."

Then Kendall reached Dylan and the service began. They'd chosen a simple service, but the familiar words rolled through Taylor with the power of tradition. "Will you take this man?"

She had, when she'd been asked the same question, but not for all that long as it turned out.

In times of health, when things were better, there'd been no problem. The minute they were hit with sickness and worse, the marriage had crumbled.

Till the first sign of trouble do us part.

When she heard the words, "I now pronounce you man and wife," Taylor took refuge in the embroidered handkerchief Kendall's mother had given her as a keepsake.

"This is a perfect wedding," Taylor said, hugging the bride.

"I couldn't have done it without you and Mike," she said, hugging back.

Suddenly, the subterfuge, the days spent shopping and tasting wedding delicacies and inspecting cakes, were worth every minute and calorie.

"I know you will be very happy." They would, too, she was certain. Taylor could tell when they looked at each other that what they had going was the real thing.

The receiving line was another casual affair. The invited guests who stopped to congratulate the newlyweds included most of the Winfield racing team, the pit team, some of the office staff, other NASCAR drivers, Kendall's family and a few friends from Oregon, and a few of Dylan's people.

She'd imagined feeling sorry for his parents being robbed of the fancy wedding they'd so wanted, but two minutes in their company was enough to cure her of that weakness. Dylan's parents wandered around looking richer than everybody else—not an easy feat when the ground was thick with NASCAR drivers— better dressed and superior. The younger version of Dylan's mother turned out to be his sister.

Taylor was quite ready to despise her when she saw the woman kiss Kendall and, speaking low enough that her mother couldn't hear, said, "If I ever get married; you are organizing the wedding. I've never seen my parents so neatly outmaneuvered." Then, much louder, she said, "Welcome to the family. Pull down the emergency bar, honey, the roller coaster is pulling out of the station."

Dylan turned in time to hear the last part. He put an arm around Kendall. "She can handle us." He cut a glance to his parents, who were standing with Gordon Winfield. "All of us."

"I am so happy for you," she said, hugging Dylan with much more warmth than his mother had managed. "Be happy, bro."

Dylan had chartered a friend's yacht and they were spending a short honeymoon sailing in the Bahamas before flying back in time for next weekend's race.

A hugely pregnant woman floated over to Dylan. She looked so delicate and ethereal that it was hard to imagine her small frame carrying a child, but her belly went before her proudly.

"Ashlee, honey, should you be traveling?" she heard Dylan say to the woman. Behind her stood a stolid-looking young man who hovered adorably, looking both protective and proud.

"No, she shouldn't. I told her, the doctor told her, her mother told her." He shrugged in a helpless way that suggested to Taylor that his wife wasn't one to listen to advice even when it was excellent.

"The baby's not due for a whole month, and I could not miss your second wedding." She dimpled adorably. "I was there at the first one, after all."

"She was the bride," Kendall whispered to Taylor. Kendall didn't seem at all bothered by the obvious devotion between the former spouses, smiling fondly when they embraced.

"You don't mind them kissing in front of you?"

"Are you kidding? It's because of Ashlee that we met." She smiled as though at a really good memory. "I was Dylan's date for his ex-wife's wedding."

"I can't imagine," Taylor said.

"Neither can I," said Mike, standing at her side. "Poor fool should have stayed away."

"It's a long story. I'll tell you sometime. Trouble was, Ashlee still thought she was in love with Dy and spent a lot of effort trying to get him back."

"Ah, didn't you say you met her at her wedding?"

Kendall chuckled. "Like I said, it's a long story. Since she realized she's in love with her husband and not mine, life's been easier for all of us."

"I bet."

Kendall gasped. "Did you hear that? I called Dylan my husband." She laughed. "First time ever. But Ashlee's a good person. And I think being a mother will suit her perfectly."

When Ashlee and Dylan let go of each other, the mom-to-be shrieked at the sight of Kendall. "Oh, honey, you look beautiful."

"Thank you." They hugged and Taylor enjoyed

the spectacle of Dylan's former and brand-new wives embracing.

Dylan and his ex-wife obviously had a good relationship even though they'd both moved on to other people.

She wondered if she and Mike would be able to do that. She turned toward him, but found him talking to the beautiful young wife of a driver. No, she thought, as she gazed at him, which caused the usual mix of emotions swirling around inside of her, she didn't think they would ever have an easy friendship.

CHAPTER SIXTEEN

TAYLOR HAD LONGED FOR and dreaded this day in equal measure.

Once the receiving line broke up and the guests enjoyed canapés and champagne, it was time for the wedding photos. The formal soon morphed into informal as Dylan and Kendall called family and guests over for a photo.

Carl Edwards strolled by looking surprisingly formal in a suit. "Carl," Kendall squealed in a most un-Kendall-like way. "I want a picture with Carl."

His blue eyes twinkled as he hooked one arm around Kendall's waist and another around Dylan's shoulders. The three of them grinned into the camera. After the shutter had clicked a couple of times, Kendall hugged Carl.

"If you hadn't given me advice on dating a driver, I might not be here today," she said.

"If I'd taken my own advice, I might not have so many ex-girlfriends." He shook his head in mock sadness, but Taylor thought he looked pretty happy with his life.

He shook hands with Dylan. "Congratulations."

"Thanks."

"I hope I get a dance with the bride," Carl said. "Since I kind of brought you two together."

"Absolutely."

"Cool."

As he walked away, Kendall sighed. "It's a good thing I fell in love with you, first," she said to her new husband.

"Good thing for me, too."

Dinner was served under the big tent, and Taylor sat at the head table and gazed out at guys she usually saw in racing uniforms and helmets looking quite different in formal wear and fresh haircuts.

Mike was the best man and also the MC and she thought Dylan couldn't have chosen better. He was funny, but not stand-up-comedian steal-the-show funny, and he kept things on track. Even though they weren't married anymore, she couldn't help feeling proud of him.

Not even Mike could dim the pinging of cutlery against glasses and Kendall and Dylan didn't seem too upset about the number of times they had to stop and kiss each other.

Mike rose and said, "Every bride needs someone to support her on the big day. Kendall chose Taylor Robinson and, in my humble opinion, she couldn't have chosen better."

She'd forgotten there was a toast to the bridesmaids—in this case only her—and it hadn't occurred to her that the best man would be giving that toast. The etiquette books pegged the groom for that job, but when Kendall had told her that Dylan, who wasn't at all afraid to drive at 180 miles an hour around a track, was hopeless at preparing a formal speech, she'd assumed they'd forgo the toasts.

Now it was Mike toasting her. When he uttered the words he looked right at her and she felt a shiver run along her skin. He looked so serious, so sweet. She tried not to blush, but she had a feeling she was pinker than the roses in Kendall's bouquet.

"I've had a chance to get to know Taylor since we've been involved in this wedding, and I'm getting to know a woman who is smart, goal-oriented and makes the best of things."

He then recounted a mildly amusing story about pew bows that hadn't seemed funny at the time. The florist had forgotten them and the van had roared off to pick them up, arriving only minutes before the ceremony. Taylor had given a near-hysterical Kendall strict orders to sit down, preferably with her head between her knees, and then had calmly borrowed two rolls of sticky tape from the Winfields' housekeeper. She'd given Mike one roll, taken the other, and as guests were arriving, the sound of scritching could be heard as the two of them taped the bows to the rows of chairs in the garden.

"I like to think that a woman like that is a good one to have around. Can I just say, on a personal note, that I also think she looks gorgeous."

There was enthusiastic clapping from a couple of the NASCAR tables and an ear-piercing whistle that she rather thought came from Hank's direction, but she never took her gaze off Mike's. She couldn't. Her blush deepened.

"Ladies and gentleman, please join me in a toast to the maid of honor. To Taylor."

Glasses rose all around. "To Taylor."

After the dinner and speeches were done, dancing began. Taylor spent most of her time feeling like a chaperone at a high-school dance. She was worried that Hank was going to do someone an injury, he danced so wildly. Fortunately, Louise Hunnicut, if she couldn't keep him in line, could certainly keep up with him.

Taylor stood there watching them, smiling to herself when she considered how Hank had planned to sport a gorgeous model or starlet on his arm at every race and how quickly he'd become a one-woman man. They made a striking couple. Louise, with makeup on, her hair up and wearing a stylish dress, was gorgeous. Hank, looking pretty good himself—when he wasn't dancing—was obviously smitten.

Taylor had no idea how serious the romance would become, but she was thankful the woman didn't own a teacup Chihuahua. Now that he had Louise in his life, Hank had less time to devote to stupid pranks, like arranging for Mike to take his place as Dylan's stand-in groom.

She was watching Hank and Louise dance so closely it was practically illegal when a voice said in her ear, "I take a lot of pride in that romance. It's the only match I ever made."

She glanced over her shoulder at Mike. "You introduced them so you could get a story."

One side of his mouth kicked up. "Yeah, but I still got them together. I get points."

"Not many."

"Care to join them?"

She nodded and melted into Mike's arms. There was something so magical about this night. The music, the happiness flowing around them, the feel of the man she had loved so passionately moving with her on the dance floor.

"Feels weird, doesn't it?" Mike said in her ear.

"Being at a wedding?"

He nodded, his cheek brushing her hair. "It brings back memories."

"Some of them are even good."

"Sorry I was such a lousy husband."

She sighed and laid her head on his shoulder. "You weren't so bad. Sorry I was such a lousy wife."

"You weren't so bad, yourself."

TAYLOR MADE SURE TO STAY out of the way when Kendall threw the bouquet.

"Don't you want a shot at catching the flowers?" Hank asked her as she joined the married women and the hooting men. Hank was watching

Louise, who was part of the giggling group of single women.

"I want to catch that bouquet about as much as I want to catch flesh-eating disease."

Once the bride and groom headed out in a limo on the way to the airport, the reception turned into an all-out party.

Dylan had hired a firm to make sure everybody who drank got a drive home, and the party was well under control between the catering staff and the Winfields. Which meant that Taylor was off the hook.

About midnight, she was thinking of heading out when she found Mike behind her. "Hey, pretty lady, can I give you a ride home?"

He gestured behind him to where a town car was waiting, a uniformed chauffeur holding open the door.

"I could get used to this," she said, as she slid into the backseat of the luxurious car.

"Marry a driver and you can."

She laughed. "Most of them are taken."

"Hank Mission's single. If you could keep him off the dance floor he's not a bad guy."

She turned to him in the dim light, seeing his eyes darker and more intense than usual. Was it possible he was feeling a little insecure? Mike who never cared about material possessions? Or was he jealous?

"Hank's my boss. Not my boyfriend."

"Okay."

"He's seeing Louise exclusively."

"Cool."

For some reason, his suggestion annoyed her. The car slid smoothly onto the highway, heading for her apartment.

"Nice party," Mike said after silence had reigned for a few minutes.

"I can't believe you would even think that of me."

"Think what?"

"That I would be interested in Hank. It would be totally unprofessional of me to date him, not to mention the fact that he's not my type—"

"He's also at least five years younger than you are."

Her irritation level notched higher. "Are you saying I'm too old for him?"

"What do you care? I thought you weren't interested in him."

"Well, if I was, I wouldn't be too old. Older women and younger men are very fashionable these days."

"Sure. Sorry I brought it up." He sounded like he couldn't care less.

She was so annoyed she felt her heart begin to hammer. "Is there something you're getting at here? I don't appreciate snide innuendoes."

She saw his head turn her way. "Did you have too much to drink or something?"

"I can't believe I was ever married to you," she said in a fierce undertone. "What was I thinking?"

"I don't think either of us were thinking."

Her jaw pretty much unhinged itself at that. "Are you deliberately trying to insult me?"

"No. What is wrong with you?"

"What's wrong with me? What's wrong with you? You used to think I was pretty hot, buddy. All I had to do was flick my hair and you were mine."

"Yeah. That was a while ago."

Was he really that immune or was he trying to bait her? She was so riled she couldn't tell. But there was one way to find out.

"So, if I flicked my hair right now, it would have no effect?"

"Well, your hair's a lot shorter. And it's pretty dark."

"And if I undid the buttons on my dress, I guess that wouldn't matter because you couldn't see."

"You could tell me what you were doing," he said, his voice slowing and deepening. "I've got a pretty good imagination."

"And you'd feel nothing?" she shrieked.

"I didn't say that."

Anger was turning into something else, something she really didn't want to think about right now.

There was only one way to put this guy in his place once and for all. She leaned over and kissed him, right on his arrogant, goading, lying mouth.

Even as her brain shouted, *Bad idea*, her mouth found his and it was so familiar, still so hot between them, that she was startled by the blast of lust that roared through her system.

She was in his arms and he was pulling her against him, their mouths hungry for each other, hands reaching, grasping.

They were barely aware that the car had stopped. The door opened and the very correct chauffeur stood politely, eyes gazing into the distance as they dragged themselves out of the interior with a quick word of thanks.

They didn't run, but they walked pretty fast to get to her apartment. No words were exchanged. No invitation issued, no permission asked. They reached the door and she fumbled open the lock, almost dropping her keys when he slid his warm palm along her arm.

Once inside, she led him straight to her bed. Their need for each other was so strong, she felt like her skin was on fire. They knew each other so well that there was no fumbling or uncertainty. This was so familiar, and yet somehow new.

She could barely make out his features in the dim light of the moon shining into her bedroom, but she felt his fierce concentration. Tasted his need when they kissed.

She fell back into the greatest passion she'd ever known.

When at last they curled together to sleep, she thought it was the most content she'd felt in a couple of years.

CHAPTER SEVENTEEN

MIKE OPENED HIS EYES, wondering first where he was and second why he felt so bone-deep good. He turned his head on the pillow and there was Taylor sprawled beside him sound asleep, taking up more of the bed than any woman of her size ought to be able to.

He, of course, was pushed to the edge of the mattress. It was all so familiar, he couldn't keep the smile off his face. How had he missed being shoved around in sleep by a woman half his size? He looked at her, her face relaxed, and he felt a painful twist in his chest. How had they screwed this up so badly?

He watched her for a bit, simply enjoying the moment and the fact that, amazingly, they were here again. So, he knew one thing for sure, she was still as hot for him as he was for her. It was all he knew, but it was a start.

Thinking over the events of the past few hours, he decided it was a damned fine start.

He'd always been the earlier riser of the two, so

he proceeded to fall back into the morning routine of their marriage. He rolled out of bed carefully so as not to wake her and watched, amused, as she stretched her leg out to claim the spot he'd occupied. She could spread herself out on a queen-size bed the way most people would cover a twin.

When they moved back in together, he thought, they'd have to invest in a king-size mattress. Then he thought, nah, he preferred the intimacy of the queen. While he was puttering around finding where she kept the coffee stuff, and then putting a pot together, it hit him. He was already thinking of them getting back together.

He blinked against the steam as he sipped his first coffee of the day. The caffeine gave him a second jolt. Wow. Was it just a great night that had him thinking of putting himself back with a woman who had caused him so much grief?

He carried his coffee to the front door to get the paper he knew he'd find outside, then, realizing he was naked, backtracked to the bathroom where he grabbed Taylor's white cotton robe off the hook. It didn't reach his knees, and since his ex-wife was definitely a lot slimmer in the middle than he was, he barely made it to decent. He opened the door cautiously, stuck his head around it, and then, seeing no one in the hallway, stooped for the paper.

As though he'd done it a thousand times before, which was not far from the truth, he topped up his own coffee, poured a second mug with a big slurp of skim milk in it, tucked the paper beneath his arm and carried the works back to the bedroom.

Her furniture was sparse to the point of monastic and the collection didn't boast bedside tables, so he put her coffee on top of the stack of books that sat by her side of the bed. As he straightened, he found her eyes opened and on him, with the unfocused expression of the barely awake.

He leaned down and gave her a quick kiss. "Morning, sunshine."

She blinked. "You are wearing my robe."

"I was bringing it to you. Didn't have a free hand."

With great good humor, he slipped out of the thing and laid it beside her on the bed. Then, in spite of a strong desire to pick up where they'd left off last night, he knew from experience he'd get nowhere until she'd downed her first cup of coffee. So, he walked around and climbed into the other side of the bed, splitting the paper in two and handing her the front end. He'd start with the sports and leisure while she took the news and then they'd switch. He could read and, at the same time, keep an eye on the level of her coffee mug. He was hopeful that if he timed it right they'd do more than read the paper.

When she didn't immediately take her section of paper he looked up and found that she was trying to put on her robe without exposing her body. "What are you doing?"

"Putting on my robe," she said.

"There's nothing under there that I haven't already seen," he reminded her. "And wouldn't mind seeing again, real soon."

She fumbled the belt around her and then sat up carefully, as though she were a Christmas present wrapped tightly so as to keep the surprise until Christmas morning.

Some of his sprightly mood began to ebb.

Taylor had never been particularly shy about her body, and she had to know how much he loved it. So what was going on?

She reached for her coffee, sipping it slowly and staring straight ahead, not even pretending to read the front page.

He was tempted to retreat into the sports section and let her do her mulling in private, but some instinct told him that this was not a time to let her be. It was a time to poke. So, he uttered a line he'd probably never uttered before in his life. "Do you want to talk about something?"

When she turned and stared at him, her eyes wide and full of disbelief, he wished he'd followed his first inclination. He could be reading about a game that had simple rules, an obvious way of keeping track of what was going on and a clear result at the end of it. Instead, he was treated to his ex-wife and new lover looking at him as if he'd just spoken in a language she'd never heard before.

"Do I want to talk about something?" she echoed.

"You seem kind of uptight."

She turned to him. "I spent the night with my ex-husband. I feel uptight."

From the pleasure of being together again and the deep sleep that had followed, she should be feeling very, very relaxed. He did not, however, point that out. Instead he waited.

She made a sound between a groan and a howl and put her hands over her face. "I must have been out of my mind."

"Not that I want you to give a thought to my male ego, but this is not exactly flattering."

She ignored his attempt at humor. "I can't believe we were so stupid."

"Oh, good. That's a lot better."

That got a reluctant chuckle out of her. She flopped down onto her back and rolled to face him, looking a lot more like her real self and much less like a newly created zombie. "It was stupid."

"There are a lot of words I could use to describe last night," he said, laying a hand over hers where it rested on the bed. "*Stupid* is not one of them."

For a second her eyes softened. "It's not the sleeping together. That's always been great between us. It's everything else. Mike, we broke up. We got a divorce. We are not supposed to sleep together."

"Are you saying round two is out of the question?"

She rolled the other way, right out of the bed. "I'm saying any round is out of the question. It was a mistake," she muttered as she picked up her coffee and stalked to the kitchen. "Mistakes happen."

He got out and followed her, arriving in time to see her top up her mug with a hand that was a little shaky. "We pretend it never happened. We move on."

"Why would we do that?"

She turned around and glared at him. "Would you put some clothes on?"

This morning really wasn't going the way he'd hoped it would. He took his time finding his clothes where they were flung all over the place. He came back with his dress pants on and his shirt. While he buttoned the latter he said, "Half our problem has been pretending things never happened that did. Maybe we should sit down and talk about this."

For a second she looked so vulnerable he wanted to take her in his arms. "I think it's too late." Her hand slipped to her belly.

He snorted with disbelief. "Last night was up there with the best nights of my life. You want to talk about that?"

He waited for the words to register, and for the telltale pink to stain her cheeks. She shook her head.

"How about this. I know we made mistakes before. We took what we had for granted and it was easy. Then it got hard and we both bailed. If I could go back I'd handle things differently." There was so much he wanted to say to her, but he didn't know how to begin, how to tread ground that he knew was painful.

For a long moment they stared at each other. He was looking for some cue, some acknowledgment that it was okay for him to keep talking, to take them down the road they really needed to travel. As though warning him to stop, she shook her head.

"Taylor, we didn't talk when we should have. The counselor I saw said—"

Her gaze snapped to his face. "You saw a counselor?"

He wished he hadn't brought it up. He felt stupid admitting he'd needed help. Baring his troubles to strangers had never been his style. "Yeah."

"Reena will be impressed."

"Reena?"

Taylor bit her lip. "She thinks we both should go."

He'd always liked Reena. He was liking her more by the second. "Okay."

Her eyes were clouded with doubts. "You're saying you would go with me to a counselor and talk about all the things that caused us to break up?"

"Absolutely."

For a long moment there was silence. He heard the fridge rumble and somewhere outside a truck drove by.

"I need to think about this. Probably you should go home," she said, her voice sounding husky and uncertain. She found a spoon and started stirring her coffee as though the future of the human race depended on perfectly blended skim milk and coffee.

"Taylor," he said, wanting her to look up at him at least, but her attention remained focused on her coffee.

"Please."

There was another aeon of silence. Once more he felt his old helplessness around her. She shut him out and he didn't know how to get past the barricades she put around her emotions. He wanted to kick them down, but he was afraid of making things worse.

Fool, he cursed himself. Getting caught up in this net of confusion once more.

He stalked back into the bedroom, shoved on the one sock he could find, and his shoes. He stuffed his bow tie and cummerbund in a pocket, then stomped back to the kitchen where she was still standing where he'd left her.

How could she be so stubborn?

"If you won't talk to me, then here's something you can think about," he said as he walked down the tiny hallway to her front door. He opened it and turned. She'd followed him as he'd known she would. She was a few feet away, close enough to talk to but not close enough to touch.

He ached, having to leave her. She had the tousled, heavy-eyed look of a woman who's been well loved. Her feet were bare and under her robe was the body he knew so well and so intimately. He wanted nothing more than to go back in there and muss her up some more. But he couldn't. She'd told him to leave.

Maybe he couldn't stay, but there was something he needed to tell her. Something that was going to surprise her as much as it had surprised him when it hit him this morning.

He looked her straight in the eye. "I want you back."

She took a step back so fast it was more like she jumped.

"I'll do whatever I have to do to make it happen."

CHAPTER EIGHTEEN

MIKE was still steaming when he got outside and realized with a string of muttered curses that his car was at Dy's place.

He didn't have his cell phone with him to call a cab or a friend, and he'd be damned if he'd go back and beg Taylor for a ride to his car, so he walked out to the dusty highway and started stalking backward in the general direction of Dy's place with his thumb out.

His fantastic night had turned into a glum morning. He wanted his wife back and she was basically telling him in no uncertain terms that she didn't want him.

His sockless foot was already developing a blister as his heel rubbed the hard leather of his new dress shoe. Great. Just great.

As dark as his mood was, it wasn't completely black.

He had secret information. Something she didn't know she'd given away. As she was drifting off to sleep last night with her head on his shoulder and her hand resting on his belly, he'd whispered, "Night Tay."

"Night. Love you." The words had been uttered as she rolled off the edge of waking and tumbled into sleep, but he'd heard them loud and clear. She wouldn't ever have uttered them consciously, not under torture. But her semiconscious mind had given him the goods.

She still loved him.

The day was gearing up to be a scorcher. Dy and Kendall would be on a beach somewhere about now, hopefully getting on a lot better than their maid of honor and best man, and somewhere a nice dark sports bar with a big-screen TV was calling his name.

He could think better with a game blaring above him. And he was a man with some thinking to do. He had to figure out how to put a marriage back together, one he'd helped break apart.

He had no idea how long it was going to take him to find a pay phone or hitch a ride. He plodded along the edge of the highway, turning and extending his thumb when he heard traffic approach. He received stares of disdain, pity and amusement from the drivers and passengers of the cars and trucks who'd so far roared by him, but no one had even slowed for the unshaven dude in the tux limping along the highway at ten in the morning.

The air was dusty and his shiny new black dress shoes weren't made for hiking. He slipped out of his tux jacket and slung it over his shoulder. At least being out here gave him time to think. There was something hypnotic about plodding down an endless strip of asphalt.

He was feeling thirsty, hungry and irritable when a shiny red pickup came into view. If he'd had time to react, he'd have thrown himself into the bushes at the side of the road and hidden until the vehicle roared by. But even as he was yanking in his thumb hoping the driver wouldn't notice him, the truck wheeled to a stop a few feet in front of him. He had no choice but to walk forward and open the passenger door.

"Hey, Hank," he said, when he gazed into the grinning face of his ex-wife's boss and all-around practical joker.

"Where ya headed?"

"I left my car at Dy's. I need to go pick it up."

"Hop in. Good thing I was at Louise's last night or I wouldn't be on this highway this morning. Lucky, eh?"

"Yeah. Thanks." What could he do? He climbed in and decided to take the conversational high road. A NASCAR driver and a NASCAR columnist would always have a lot to talk about, and a certain blond hottie was not one of the topics on the table. "So, how are you feeling about your rookie season?"

Hank, however, did not seem inclined to take the conversational high road. His conversational style had a lot in common with his driving. Quick, sneaky and no-holds-barred. "Feeling fine. A man walking down the road in last night's tux has to be feeling pretty fine, also."

"Yep. There were some cute waitresses there last night."

"Sure were. Some pretty cute PR managers, too."

"I hope I remembered to get her number," he said desperately, rooting in his pockets.

Hank glanced over, a gleam of unholy amusement in his eyes. "I have her number if you need it."

They stared at each other for a second and Mike knew he was busted. He blew out a breath. "You're not going to make trouble over this, are you?"

Hank appeared to think about it while the truck cruised down the highway and Metallica boomed out from a top-of-the-line sound system.

"Here's the deal," he said at last. "I like Taylor. She's a fantastic woman and a terrific PR manager. Anybody messes with her, they'll have to deal with me."

Great. Macho swagger was exactly what he needed on top of everything else today.

Well, he was getting good at saying what he meant today even if it did have disastrous results. The truck swung down a side road and silence reigned until they reached Dylan's place and pulled up beside Mike's car.

He got out. He turned back as he was about to shut the truck's passenger door. "Here's my deal," he said. "I'm in love with Taylor. I plan to marry her." He took a second to enjoy the blank look of shock on Hank's face. "Thanks for the ride. Have a nice day."

HOW DOES A MAN GO ABOUT getting his wife back?
Mike pondered this question as he went through the
rest of his day.

There was wooing, flowers, candlelit dinners and
all that schmaltzy stuff he'd never been much good
at. But he supposed he could give it a try if it would
help him get his wife back.

Then there was the history between them, the
messy emotional drama that had broken them apart.
Before they could have a marriage that could work
they needed to play out the last act of the drama. The
resolution.

Not all the flowers and candlelit dinners in the
world could get them back together until they'd con-
fronted the elephants that had taken to stampeding
through their Seattle living room.

He thought about how he was going to get his wife
back while he de-tuxed and showered. He thought
about it while he did a few minimal chores. He thought
about it while he watched that game he'd promised
himself at his local watering hole over a burger.

By the time he was home, he'd figured out a
simple strategy. Since they'd met again here in Charlotte, he and Taylor had pretended to be strangers. He
was getting pretty tired of pretending. Now he'd
come right out and told her that he wanted her back
and he'd taken the second step of telling Hank
Mission that he was in love with the woman, perhaps
his best course of action was to keep right on going.
Go public with his courting.

Taylor would hate being wooed in public, which, in an odd way, cheered him to no end. Maybe what Taylor needed was to realize that he loved her to his marrow and always would. If he pursued her in a loud, public way, as humiliating as that might turn out to be, she'd have to tell him to go away in an equally loud, public way.

He was either going to end up as a big winner or he was going to make such a huge fool of himself that he could never show his face around NASCAR again.

He thought about it a little longer and decided that Taylor was more important than any job, any life-style. He'd started over before when she broke his heart. He figured, if he had to, he'd do it again.

He really, really hoped he wouldn't have to.

If she loved him as he had to believe, and he loved her as he knew he did, then he needed a strategy to get them back together.

TAYLOR COULDN'T REMEMBER the last time she'd been so mad at herself. Well, she waffled between being angry with herself, furious with Mike and basically snarly with fate for throwing them together again.

When her phone rang around seven that night she was tempted not to answer it, having a shrewd idea who was on the other end. But if she didn't pick up, he was perfectly capable of calling over and over again, of barraging her with funny e-mails or, as he'd done one time when they were both in Seattle, of carrying on a conversation with her through the personal ads.

Her lip quivered as she remembered the incident.

Monday: DLH (desperately lonely husband) seeks WOHD (woman of his dreams) for apology, conversation and MUS.

Only Mike would manage to slip makeup sex into a personal ad.

Naturally, she'd ignored him and pretended she hadn't read the classifieds. Didn't matter. He was undeterred.

Tuesday: Will grovel in exchange for quiet evening in front of fire.
Wednesday: I'm sorry.
Thursday: If you forgive me, meet me at our place, Friday night at 7:00.
Friday: I love you.

What could she do? Friday after work she'd walked into the sports bar where they'd spent so many Sundays watching NASCAR races. Mike was there with a big bowl of their favorite nachos. Standing up in the cheese was a single long-stemmed red rose. Of course, the rose couldn't stand up by itself in a Natcho mountain, so he'd used menus to prop the flower up. It was the lamest, not to mention messiest, flower she'd ever received. She smiled at the memory and maybe that's what made her pick up.

"Hello?"

"I missed you today."

Oh, how did he do that to her? She was a mess. He'd ruined her day, her newspaper career, her life, and yet her belly quivered at the sound of his voice. He'd said he wanted her back and a tiny bit of her believed him, but she knew Mike as well as anyone. If there was one thing he loved it was games.

However, she was no longer a woman who played games. She'd grown up. Painfully, slowly, but she'd done it. She was an adult and she needed an adult male in her life.

"I can't do this again."

"I had an interesting drive back to my car," he said as though she hadn't spoken. It was the first time she'd realized he hadn't had his car at her place. All those miles to travel and she was certain he'd had no cell phone with him. In spite of herself she said, "Oh, no. You should have come back. I'd have driven you to your car."

"A seven-mile walk was easy compared to having you glare at me again."

She groaned aloud. "I didn't mean to glare. It wasn't your fault. Entirely. It's just that sleeping with you was such a bad idea."

"Too bad you feel that way. Sleeping with you was the best idea I've had in a long time."

In spite of herself she was caught. "Really?"

"Yep."

They were divorced. But her lips didn't seem to care about the warnings coming from her brain. "How long?"

"You mean how long since I've had a…good idea like that?"

Did she even want to know? He was one of those guys who drew women not with macho good looks but with his great sense of humor and charm that she'd fallen for before she'd realized she was in danger. Once she'd gone, he must have had plenty of opportunities for companionship. She squeezed her eyes shut and then found she did want to know. "Yes."

"You won't laugh?"

"No."

"Fourteen months."

Okay, so math wasn't her strong point, but even she could figure out this equation. "You haven't had any…ideas since we split up?"

"Nope. And it does my ego no good to admit that."

She could imagine. He was such a guy's guy. When she'd first met him he always had a woman around. He was popular, funny, cute in that cuddly way he had. She'd assumed she was another in a string of women until one day she woke up to find her feelings were serious. His must have been, too, because next thing she knew they were vacationing together.

In Hawaii. Beach-wedding capital of the world.

How did it feel to find out that Mike hadn't been with anyone since she'd left?

It felt weird. Scary. But also nice.

She knew he wanted to ask her, she could feel the question ebbing and flowing between them. She was a fool to let him know she'd been celibate, too, but she'd always been a fool where he was concerned.

In spite of the fact that she'd warned herself not to encourage him, she said, "I haven't had any ideas, either, since we split up."

She heard his breath huff out as he expelled it. "Thank God."

She laughed shakily. "Which is probably why we both acted so crazy last night. This is still a bad idea and way too complicated."

"Guess what makes it even more complicated?"

A sixth sense told her she didn't want to know. Again, her mouth took over from her common sense. "What?"

"I hitchhiked to my car."

"In your tux?"

"Yep. Guess who picked me up?"

Her stomach started to sink. "I'm not going to like it, am I?"

"I didn't like it myself. It was Hank."

She'd guessed it was bad, but not that bad. "Oh, no." Her hand tightened on the phone so hard she got a cramp. "You didn't tell him you'd been with me, did you?"

"Didn't have to. He's smarter than he looks."

"Oh, no. Oh, no, oh, no, oh, no." She breathed. This was not a disaster. "You didn't confirm anything, right? I mean, he can guess all he wants, but if neither of us give him any—"

"I tried to bluff it out but he busted me."

"Wh-what did you do? Tell me you didn't confirm his suspicion."

"I told him I'm in love with you."

"You did what?" She felt a bubble of hysteria rising in her chest. He had to be kidding. Please let him be kidding.

"I'm tired of playing games. I felt like telling the truth."

"But what about my career? My job? My reputation? I just started there this year, I don't want—"

"Last time I looked it didn't hurt a woman's rep to have a man in love with her."

"You don't understand—"

"We don't even work for the same company. Getting together when we worked for the same paper was a lot more complicated, but we worked it out. This is not a big deal."

It was a big deal to her. A big, scary, messy, bad deal. "I don't have time for this."

"It's true. I am still in love with you."

"Well, I'm not—"

"Don't say it," he ordered her. "Just don't say it."

"But—"

"I have an idea."

She was still reeling from his declaration. She could barely focus. "What idea?"

"Why don't we go out for dinner like a civilized couple and get to know each other?"

How had she ever married someone who was so completely off his rocker? "Mike, we were married for three years. We know each other."

"See, that's what I'm figuring out. I spent a lot of time thinking today. We never did know each other. Not really. I think we should start over."

It didn't even sound like him. To talk about them not knowing each other before meant he'd been thinking about their marriage, not simply running from the bad memories. She sank to the floor and sat cross-legged, her back leaning against her couch. "Start over."

"Yes. Like people who've just met. We'll date, we'll talk, we'll—"

"You want to date your ex-wife?"

"I want more than that, but I'll start with a date. Dinner, any night you say."

"Oh, Mike. I don't know."

"Think about it. I'm not going anywhere."

She couldn't sit still. She rose from the floor, paced across her small living area feeling confused, miserable and a little hopeful. "I'm not promising anything. But I'll think about it."

CHAPTER NINETEEN

TAYLOR HAD A COUPLE of hours to kill at the track in Indianapolis. Hank was napping in his motor home, and she felt like being out with the race fans simply enjoying the day. As she made her way to pit road it was like passing 150,000 walking billboards for drivers and their sponsors.

Every time she passed somebody wearing a Hank Mission shirt, jacket or hat she felt like patting the fan on the back and telling them they had great taste.

Fans were getting their photos taken with the pit teams of their favorite drivers. The pre-race excitement was as bright as the sun overhead.

"You look happy about something."

She hadn't noticed Mike in the crowd. He was leaning against a stack of tires. His notebook was out and he'd obviously been getting some local color. Whether he'd been interviewing fans or pit team guys, it was impossible to guess. Mike liked to talk to all kinds of people, and one of his favorite rules for soft features was that instead of finding the story, he let the story find him. She guessed that was how he kept his column so fresh and the readers coming back for more.

If she'd known he'd be out here, she'd have hidden in the hauler and caught up on e-mail or something. She hadn't seen Mike since he'd walked out of her apartment in bits and pieces of his tux.

And she still hadn't given him her answer about dinner. She appreciated that he was giving her the space she needed to figure out her answer, because she knew that when he invited her for dinner, he was really asking her if there was any chance of them getting back together.

The answer to that was a mystery, so she hadn't called.

Since they were staring at each other and he was walking toward her it was impossible to pretend she hadn't seen him and keep on going. So she stood her ground and answered his question. "I like walking pit road. It gets me psyched for the race."

"Mind if I walk with you?"

Screaming "Yes" seemed childish, so she shook her head and he fell into step with her.

"It's a good crowd," she said, sending him a strong signal that this was her workplace and all conversation should be racing related.

"You've been avoiding me," he replied, sending her an equally strong message, she supposed, that he was going to talk about personal issues whether she wanted to or not. How typical.

"I've been busy."

"See, that's avoidance. You can always find time for somebody you want to talk to."

"Well, there you have it. You have seen right through me." She threw up her hands. "You're right. I don't want to talk to you."

She increased her pace, dodging a tour group and squeezing past a family of six. The youngest, a little girl, dragged her feet and plucked at her Dylan Hargreave T-shirt as though she wished it were a sparkly Barbie outfit. Poor kid. Taylor couldn't help but smile down at her.

Mike, being Mike, didn't slow his steps and disappear into the crowd; he stuck to her side, following her gaze when she smiled at the little girl.

"You really like kids," he said as though it were news.

She turned to him, wondering what would make him say anything so stupid. "Have you got sunstroke or something?"

"No. I'm trying to strike up a conversation."

"How's it going on your end? 'Cause I have to tell you, on my end you're closer to striking out."

"Ah, sports terminology. Excellent way to communicate with a jock reporter." He tipped the bill of his cap as a trio of marines walked by. "Come on, give me a break. I'm here, you're here. We've got some time before we have to go to work. Let's spend it together."

"What happened to the part where I said I don't want to talk to you?"

"I think you do."

"But you are a monumental egotist."

"Taylor, I've known you for a while. Pretty intimately, I might add." She glared at him, but he continued without a pause. "If you were done with me completely and irrevocably you'd have said so."

She stared off in the distance at the banked siding of Turn Two, which was quiet now but would see a lot of action in a few hours. Above them, bleachers rose toward the sky. Already, scattered fans were seated, playing cards or chatting to while away the time. "I thought I was," she said softly.

"I know. I thought so, too." He sighed heavily. "When I saw you again, I don't know, it felt like we'd been together the day before, you know?"

She nodded. She did know. "Bumping into you was one of the bigger shocks of my life."

"Thought I might have a heart attack."

"We handled it pretty well, though. I don't think anyone suspected anything." Her forehead creased into a frown. "At least, not until—"

"Not until Hank caught me at ten in the morning walking away from your place. Then, I told him I'm in love with you. I'm guessing he might suspect something." He glanced at her sideways. "Has he said anything to you?"

"No. Not a word." Her frown deepened. "Which is very unlike him. If I end up the butt of one of his practical jokes, you will be a dead man."

"Hank's a good guy. He wouldn't do anything to

embarrass you. I don't think." But he didn't sound too sure. "Do you want me to talk to him? Tell him not to blab?"

"I can't think of anything I'd like less. I don't want Hank getting involved in my personal life." She upped her pace as they neared Hank's spot on pit road. "Maybe he thought you were joking."

When she realized he was not responding, not even still in step with her, she turned to find him rooted to the spot. "Isn't that your little gal pal?" he asked.

She followed the direction of his gaze and saw what he was looking at. The little girl who'd been following behind her family plucking at her T-shirt was standing all alone. She stood stock-still, search-ing all around her with a panicked expression in her eyes. "Where's her family?"

"Looks like they got separated."

They turned as one and made their way to where the little girl stood.

"Hi," Mike said, squatting down to her level. "Are you lost?"

Her anxious look intensified and her lip quivered. "Not allowed to talk to strangers," she said in a soft, scared voice.

"Of course you're not," Taylor said, also squatting down. She was thinking fast. "And you're right." They could stay exactly here and wait for her parents to find her; trouble was that with so many fans coming and going it was going to be hard for this child's parents to spot one little girl in this crowd.

Mike glanced her way. She knew he was having the very same thought she was. It was spooky how they were still so in tune with each other. "I have an idea," Mike said. He pointed to Dylan Hargreave on the child's T-shirt. "He's not a stranger, right? Dylan's on your T-shirt."

The little girl stared at Mike solemnly for a long moment, then looked down at the photo transfer of Dylan standing with his car that was on her T-shirt. "Right. My dad says he's got what it takes, so I guess that means he's a friend."

"Good. Excellent." He turned, still crouching, and pointed to where Dylan's pit stop was set up. "Can you see that box over there? There's a picture of Dylan Hargreave and the same car that's on your T-shirt."

She looked at the pit area, busy with crew and fans, then back at her T-shirt. She nodded. "Is he there?"

Mike glanced at Taylor. "Sticky point," he said. "He's probably not there, but lots of his friends are. Here's what I'm thinking. You and me and Taylor will walk over there and then we can call your parents and tell them where to find you."

She contemplated this for another minute, then nodded. The two adults rose, taking each side of her, and she raised her hands, so used to holding the hands of adults, Taylor supposed, that it didn't occur to her not to.

Taking the small, warm and slightly sticky hand in her own caused a wrench somewhere under

Taylor's breastbone. She glanced across at Mike, holding the other hand, and found him returning her gaze. This could have been them, his look said, the three of them at a race. A family. She started to calculate how old their baby would have been and then stopped herself with an act of will.

Instead, she went into chipper mode. "I know the guys on Dylan's pit crew. I bet they'll let you ask them anything you like. We could even take a picture of you with them."

This did not seem like the life's ambition of the child walking between them. She looked up at Taylor and sighed. "I like Mary Kate and Ashley better."

"The Olsen twins?" Mike said. "Isn't she kind of young?"

"They made a bunch of movies for youngsters. Now butt out."

She turned back to the child. "Does your dad make you come to the races because he's a fan?"

"Everybody in my family is a fan. Even my mom." She glanced up with a little-girl grin. "But if I come here, I get a new Mary Kate and Ashley DVD when we get home."

Taylor laughed. "I'm Taylor. This is Mike."

"Hello." She bit her lip. "I'm not supposed to tell strangers my name."

"That's okay. Your parents are really smart to teach you those rules." Smart except for the part where they lost their kid at one of the most crowded venues in America.

"Do they have cell phones?"

"Yes."

"Good. Then we can phone them."

The little girl looked up in surprise. "Do you know their number?"

Once more she and Mike shared a glance. He made a wry grimace. Right. This wasn't going to be as easy as she'd hoped.

Mike was in full protective mode, she noted, making sure their tiny charge was insulated from the pushing throngs as they got closer to Dylan's pit box.

Rapidly, Taylor explained the situation to Mike Nugent, Dylan's crew chief. He was a father himself and she knew he was great with kids. Sure enough, he didn't disappoint.

"Hi there, little lady," he said. "I have a little girl at home about your age. She's six years old."

"I'm five."

"Well now, aren't you a big girl. Listen, honey, I have an idea."

"For finding my mom?"

"Yep. How would you like to climb right on top of this box and you can look down and see if you can spot your folks?"

She gazed up. "I could do that."

"Good girl. I'll help you. You know, that's where Dylan's best friend watches the race from. That's where I watch the race from."

Taylor pulled out her cell phone. "Is it your mom or your dad who has the cell phone?"

"They both do."

Mike immediately pulled out his phone.

"Can you give us the first and last name of your mother and your father?"

She looked a bit suspicious and also uncertain. Poor kid.

The crew chief said, "I bet they are worried about you. If we phone them they can come get you right here."

"Can I still go on top of that box?"

"You sure can."

"When my family gets here will you let my brothers climb up, too?"

The crew chief was nobody's fool. "No way," he said. "This is for special guests only."

She beamed at him. "Okay. My dad's name is Lester Stiggant and my mom's name is Alice."

Mike was already punching numbers. "What are you doing? Four-one-one won't find a cell phone number."

"Maybe there's somebody home at their place, or they might have left a cell phone number on their recorded greeting. At the very least, I can leave a message so they can call me."

"I live on Bluebonnet Crescent. Number 145," the girl said proudly.

"That's great. Do you know what city that's in?"

The small face creased. "Texas?"

"Good. Texas is a great start, honey. Don't worry. We'll find your parents."

By this time, the child had been helped to the top of the pit box and was looking much happier. She and Mike Nugent were both scanning the crowd. "You're looking for a family, all decked out in Hargreave gear," Taylor told the crew chief.

"Needle, meet haystack," Mike mumbled.

She was thinking that pretty soon they were going to have to call in some help from somebody who knew more than she did about the usual procedure when a child got lost. Maybe there was a "Lost Child Center" or something. Something told her this wasn't the first time and probably wouldn't be the last.

Mike made a face. "There are a lot of Stiggants in Texas."

He stopped and they both glanced upward as a piercing scream rent the air. "Mommy!"

Now, Taylor didn't believe for a second that in a crowd that was in the tens of thousands, all milling, talking, laughing, yelling, that one child's voice could reach its target.

Already Mike was sprinting in the direction that the child had pointed, hoping no doubt to find the one family among many decked out in Hargreave wear.

Afterward, she realized that both of them had overlooked some mysterious mother instinct. Within twenty seconds, a sweating, panting woman arrived in Taylor's line of vision. Even the photo of Dylan on her shirt looked worried.

"Brittany, honey, don't move!"

Behind her jogged an overweight guy whose complexion was the color of pickled beetroot, with three boys trailing him. Mike brought up the rear.

After being helped down from the top of the pit box, Brittany was lifted by Mike over the barricade and into her mother's arms. "Oh, baby, I was so worried about you."

"I couldn't find you."

"She wasn't on her own too long," Mike Nugent said. "Taylor and Mike over there brought her here. And she was a real trouper and got up there like an eagle scout and spotted you all. Now you've been in the pit, you're an honorary member of the team," he continued, pulling out a Dylan Hargreave key chain and presenting it to the child.

"Wow. Thanks."

"I can't thank you enough for looking out for my baby," Alice Stiggant said, her breathing still ragged.

"She's a great kid," Taylor said.

"I didn't tell them my name, 'cause they were strangers. Can I tell them now?"

"Sure, honey."

"My name's Brittany Stiggant."

"Hi, Brittany." Taylor leaned closer. "I hope you get your new DVD."

"Will I still get my DVD? I was good, Mama. I didn't mean to get lost."

Her mom hugged her tight. "Of course you'll get your DVD. I'm so proud of you for being so brave."

She glanced up at Taylor. Sweat was sparking on

her forehead and she appeared close to tears. "It's your greatest fear as a mother."

Taylor nodded.

"You were great. You must have kids of your own."

Her gaze went straight to Mike's. She couldn't help it. "No. Not yet."

"Let's go get some ice cream," the woman said to her family, her daughter still clutched tight in her arms. "Mommy needs to sit down."

After the relief and thank-yous, the family left. Taylor felt adrenaline seep away. "Phew," she said. The entire drama hadn't taken half an hour, but she felt as though she'd run a marathon.

"Come on," Mike said, grabbing her hand and pulling.

"Come on where?"

"I need to do a pre-race interview."

"With me?"

"Yes."

She shook her head. "Sometimes you are such a madman."

They walked back into the crowd, thicker now as the race drew closer. "I prefer the term *eccentric*," he said, pulling out a steno pad and a pen.

She watched him, wondering what was going on in his devious brain. "You're interviewing me here?"

"Mmm. Lots of local background noise."

"But you're not taping."

He held up an imperious hand. "Please, leave the details to the professional."

She couldn't help the smile that pulled at her mouth. "I sometimes think you married me because I'm the only person who thinks you're funny."

"Lots of people think I'm funny." He raised his gaze to hers. "I married you for other reasons."

The crowds seemed to still, noise faded to silence. She hated the way he made her feel, as though she were part of him and he was part of her, especially when it was so spectacularly untrue.

She dragged her gaze away and said, "Okay, fire away."

"How did it feel to save a child today?"

"Like a tiny act of common sense. And don't be so dramatic."

"It was good to see the family put back together, though, wasn't it?"

She recalled the moment when she and Mike had been linked by the child's warm little hands and frowned. "Where are you going with this?"

He flipped his notebook closed. "Will you have dinner with me tomorrow night?"

"I'm not sure, I have to—"

"I'm tired of asking and having you skate around the issue. It's dinner. Not a life commitment."

"Why?"

"I cannot believe I am uttering these words a second time, but I think we need to talk."

He was right, she realized. They did need to talk. She'd pushed him away the morning after Dy and Kendall's wedding because she was so utterly vulnerable and so confused she couldn't think straight, but he was right, of course. Neither of them could move forward until they'd made peace with the past.

"All right."

"Excellent, let's say seven."

"Fine. Where should I meet you?"

"My place."

She blinked. "Why not a restaurant?"

"Because 'we need to talk' and 'waiters in your face every five seconds' do not go together."

"So, you're not planning to seduce me?"

He rolled his eyes. "Of course I'm planning to seduce you. I'm nuts about you and you're sexier than ever. But you can say no if you want to be that crazy." He must have seen that she was looking suspicious, for he added, "I'd try to seduce you in a restaurant, too."

A couple of memorable restaurant dinners came to mind and she knew he was right. If anything, she was probably less vulnerable in his apartment because she'd be expecting the move.

"Okay, seven. Now I have to go to work."

"Have a good one." He started to walk in the direction of the media center and she headed toward Hank's pit.

She turned back. "Oh. I need your address." How odd to be a visitor in Mike's home. But then everything about their relationship seemed odd.

CHAPTER TWENTY

OKAY, MIKE DECIDED WHEN he cut out of work early and headed for the grocery store, he had to get tonight exactly right. A nice dinner so she'd know he'd put some effort into it, but nothing that screamed pathetic loser trying to get his wife back. Which meant replacing the bouquet of red roses and some kind of blue flower with a handful of daffodils that only cost a couple of bucks. She liked daffodils, though. He remembered in Seattle how excited she'd get in February when they started showing up in the grocery stores. She always said it meant that spring was on its way. In six weeks, he'd remind her, but she refused to be daunted.

As he placed the flowers in his buggy, he realized how much daffodils reminded him of Taylor. But then there were a lot of things that reminded him of Taylor.

Foods, restaurants, pet phrases, even sports-equipment brands. No wonder he'd had to move away from Seattle to get away from his memories.

Not that it had exactly worked out.

Mike wasn't a gourmet chef but he had no patience for men who couldn't look after themselves or make a meal for a date.

He knew her well enough to recognize the signs that she wasn't sleeping well. The faint blue tinge under her lower eyelashes, the paleness of her skin. Stupid to notice, even stupider to worry that she was doing okay, but he'd already noticed that he was stupider than stupid where she was concerned.

He thought maybe some red meat would be good for her since she'd seemed so pale and chose a couple of T-bone steaks that he could grill, greens for a salad—organic, because Taylor was picky about stuff like that—a couple of potatoes to bake and a good bottle of red wine.

Dessert was fresh fruit and ice cream because he knew her favorite things.

Luckily, the cleaning lady came that morning so his place was in good shape. The sheets were clean and he'd left out his best pair on the assumption that you can't blame a guy for trying.

Once he'd set the table and stuck the daffodils in a vase he unearthed at the top of a cupboard, he showered, shaved, clipped his nails, brushed his teeth and even flossed.

When he was using his razor to neaten the hairline along the back of his neck he realized he was nervous. And he knew why.

Tonight mattered.

TAYLOR KNEW SHE WAS acting like an idiot when she changed her clothes for the third time. And this time she put on her best underwear, underwear so pretty it begged to be shown off.

What was she thinking?

But she didn't change. Her first upgrade had been from jeans and a white T-shirt to khakis and a cotton shirt that needed ironing. When she realized she looked like an ad for the Gap, she yanked it all off and went with a rare skirt—and the fact that Mike loved her legs had nothing to do with her clothing choice. She added a couple of layers of colorful tank tops and a light sweater. Perfect. Casual but a little dressy.

She picked up the set of opals she'd bought herself in Australia, and then at the last minute dropped them back into her jewelry case and chose the silver necklace and earrings Mike had bought her when she graduated from intern to real reporter.

He had known how important that moment was for her. She smiled a little as she put the set on. All her memories of him weren't bad. Not by a long shot.

But the bad ones were pretty bad. She doubted she could ever move past what had happened. That's what she had to tell him tonight. She looked at herself in the mirror and reluctantly replaced the silver with the opals. It wasn't fair to send him mixed messages. She couldn't show up wearing jewelry he'd given her and then tell him they had no hope of a future together.

So, she tucked the silver back in its box, folding the square of cotton around the necklace as though tucking a child into bed.

Driving into Charlotte, she reminded herself how important it was to be strong. Not to think about the past, or to let herself fall into her old bad patterns with Mike. He was a good man, she accepted that, and she supposed she'd always have a soft spot for him in her heart, but there could be no future for them.

She had to be very clear on that point. Keep her brain *in* control and her hormones *under* control.

When she drew up to his complex she recognized his car and felt a flutter in her stomach. She wasn't sure she was ready for this.

During the short walk to his town house door she wished she'd gone with the jeans. What was she thinking prancing around in a skirt? If she lived in town she'd have turned tail and dashed home to change, but as it was, a half hour drive and the return trip was out of the question. She tugged the skirt down as best she could and then rang the bell.

He answered promptly. He wore a black shirt she'd never seen before. He'd ditched his usual jeans, too, in favor of khakis. Pretty dressed up for him.

"You look great," he said, leaning forward and kissing her cheek.

He smelled good. Familiar. Safe. But she didn't want him to smell good and he most certainly wasn't safe. Not for her.

She walked in and thought how strange it was to be in his home as a guest. "Nice place," she said.

"Thanks. Come on, I'll show you around."

The town house was designed in a traditional layout with living room area at the front, then dining, then kitchen. The furniture was new and somehow impersonal. At a guess she'd say he went to Crate & Barrel and picked one of the display suites based on the size of his room. He hadn't bothered having their living room furniture moved from Seattle, then. The set they'd chosen together after weeks of her dragging him out to one show room after another.

The dining room set was also new, she realized as he led her through to the kitchen, and she oohed with envy over the granite countertops, top-of-the-line appliances and the tiny den area complete with gas fireplace. He'd installed a plasma TV and placed a recliner in front of it. Somehow she knew he spent most of his free time at home here.

A staircase led upstairs, presumably to bedrooms. He didn't offer to show her and she didn't ask.

"Want a beer or a glass of wine?" he asked her as she followed him into the kitchen.

"Sure. A glass of wine would be great. Thanks." It was awful to be so formal. She found she was nervous and wondered if he was, too.

He pulled out a bottle and went to a drawer for the corkscrew. She glanced in and spied cutlery she didn't recognize. One cupboard was glass-fronted, and she saw glasses that she'd never eyed before. In fact, she realized as she took a good look around, she didn't find anything familiar except the man living here.

"You didn't keep any of our stuff?"

He hesitated but only for a second. "Nope. Fresh start."

She felt a pang for all the things they'd collected together. For the sofa they'd argued about in Seattle. She'd wanted red, he'd preferred plaid. They'd settled on a green fabric they could both live with. For the wedding gifts and the stupid cow milk jug they'd bought because she hated him sticking the carton on the table in the morning.

And yet she had no right to complain. She'd walked away from it all. She always imagined their stuff and their house would be in Seattle. Everything the same.

Why?

Had she somewhere in the back of her mind imagined she could go back?

He handed her a glass of wine and she thanked him even as she felt sadness trickle through her.

Everything changes, she reminded herself. Everything.

They managed to keep up an easy conversation while she washed the greens and put the salad together and he grilled steaks and then pulled two of the biggest baking potatoes she'd ever seen out of the oven.

They sat at the dining table and that helped them

keep the slightly formal tone to things. They had no need to veer near any personal subjects with all of NASCAR to talk about. From personalities to the latest gossip—and there was always gossip—to going over some of the more remarkable races this season, they were able to keep the conversational ball rolling downhill, fast and smooth.

He didn't even bring up Hank so she was spared feeling as if they were talking shop.

It was the strangest dinner. The atmosphere was friendly, the conversation easy, the food good. But there was an undercurrent that was none of those things. Not friendly, not easy and for her not good. It was in the glances that stayed fixed a moment too long, the way he stopped talking when she raised her arms to push her hair behind her ears, the feelings running between them that she was here to deny.

When he illustrated a point with his usual extravagant hand gestures, she found herself losing the thread of conversation as she remembered how his hands had felt.

When dinner was finished he brewed coffee and, without even asking her, put on a pot of tea for her. She doubted he realized he'd fallen back into the routine.

"I got fruit and ice cream for dessert. Do you want it now or later?"

"Maybe later," she said, knowing he'd have bought that stuff specially for her. His taste in desserts ran to chocolate gooey things with millions of calories in every bite.

He passed her tea, in an unfamiliar mug that had flowers on it and which he would never have chosen. Suddenly irritation spurted through her. "Did you get a store's designer to pick out all this stuff?" She gestured around her.

Mike finished pouring his coffee before answering her. "No. I bought the place furnished. The couple got transferred to Belgium. She got a big job in a bank over there. They figured that rather than moving everything, they'd sell up here and start over."

He went to the fridge for milk, slopped some in his mug and turned back to her. "And, since I was all about starting over, I got rid of all the stuff in Seattle and moved in here."

"You didn't even keep the cow jug," she said, feeling stupid and childish but somehow hurt.

He leaned his elbows on the granite counter and cradled his mug. "Imagine how you'd have felt if I'd been the one who took off to the other side of the world and you were left behind." He met her gaze and she felt her own falter and drop.

"I never thought—"

"I couldn't stand having everything the same except you not being there."

"I wish you'd let me know. Maybe I would have…"

"Had no way of getting hold of you. You made sure of that."

She heard his hurt and knew she deserved the

pain she was feeling. She'd spent a lot of time concentrating on how he'd let her down, but not a lot considering that she'd taken off, leaving him to sort out everything.

There'd been some brief correspondence between their lawyers, but all that part had been amicable and easy. It was the emotional divorce that had been so messy.

"Who bought the house?" she asked, thinking about the place they'd been fixing up together.

"A nice couple. Both teachers."

She nodded. And after a tiny pause asked, "Did they have a family?"

"Yeah," he said, his voice rough. "Three boys."

She smiled. "That's good. That was a perfect family home." She sipped her tea and wondered how soon she could get out of there. She didn't think she had it in her to deliver the speech she'd planned to give. Suddenly, she just wanted to go home.

"So, are you okay?" Mike asked her.

"What do you mean, am I okay? Do I look sick?"

"No. I mean, you know…" He gestured with his hand in front of his abdomen as though running a scanner across his belly.

A flicker of pain gripped her own belly just for a second. "One in five pregnancies ends in miscarriage. It's no big deal," she said, quoting back the cruelest words he'd ever spoken to her.

He closed his eyes briefly, his head lowered. "If there's one thing in my life I wish I'd never said it was that. I just—I didn't know what to say. I was trying to make you feel better."

"Well, it didn't work."

"I do research. It's what I do." He met her gaze and she felt like she was looking right into him. His eyes were so dark and the usual humorous expression was missing. She wanted to look away, he seemed so sad and so raw and she didn't want that. She didn't want to see that in him, because she didn't want to be reminded of the worst time in her life.

But they were finally having the conversation that was a long time overdue, and maybe part of her healing process was getting out all the old feelings that still plagued her from time to time. Feelings that stopped her doing more than the most casual dating.

So she said something she'd been thinking for a long time. "I thought you blamed me for losing the baby."

His eyes darkened, so they appeared black. "What?"

"You told me not to fly down there and I went, anyway."

"There was nothing you could do for him. Your dad was in a coma."

"I thought he might come out of it. And in case he regained consciousness, even for a few minutes, I wanted to be there. I wanted to say goodbye. I wanted to tell him I was having a baby." She sank into the couch in his family room off the kitchen and rubbed her palm down her thigh, smoothing her skirt.

"But he never did regain consciousness. And then when I got home I had the miscarriage."

There was silence. "I never knew what to say. I still don't. I make my living with words, but I never have the words to say to you."

"I want to know you don't still blame me."

"Taylor, I never blamed you. It wasn't your fault."

"Maybe if I hadn't gone down there, it wouldn't have happened."

He sat beside her, not touching, but close. "It would have happened. That's what I was trying to say in my clumsy way. It happens. Statistically, it happens a lot."

"Having both those things happen at once, losing my dad and our baby. I didn't know it would be so hard."

"You kept saying you were fine. I didn't know what to do for you."

"I know. I guess I was in denial. I was so busy being fine, I never got around to grieving."

"So you left me."

"It seemed like you'd already left me. You were never home. And even if you were home, you were never there. You were on the computer or watching football or any sport they showed on television."

"I'm a sports reporter. I have to keep up."

It was a halfhearted excuse and they both knew it. "Televised bowling is not something you cover, Mike."

"Yeah."

"Probably I should have gone for counseling."

"Maybe I should have suggested it." He slumped back and stared at the blank screen of the plasma TV with the same attention he'd give if the Superbowl game of the century was playing. "Maybe I should have gone with you."

"I doubt it would have made a difference. We were never going to make it as a couple."

"Don't say that," he argued fiercely, turning his gaze on her once more. "Of course we would have made it. We were great together."

"Great when everything was going fine, but we fell apart the second things got tough. Mike, a marriage is about all the bad times as well as the good ones. The first time we were tested, we blew it."

His eyes darkened. "Does a coach fire a whole team if they have a bad first game? Does NASCAR get rid of a driver if they have a few bad races or a weak season?"

"No, but—"

"No. You know what a team does? It figures out what's wrong and starts practicing to fix the problem."

"Losing a baby isn't like fumbling a touchdown. It's not a problem you can fix."

He sat for a long moment staring into his coffee. "I don't think losing the baby was our problem. Our trouble was that we didn't know how to talk to each other."

"Do you think it's ever going to be any different?" Her voice was rising and she couldn't seem to stop it.

"Yeah, I do." He looked up at her with a slight curve to his lips. "We're talking now. About stuff that we should have talked about at the time. But we're talking."

She bit her lip. "I think it's too late."

"It's not too late. You know how I feel. I love you. When I saw you again I knew I'd never stopped. I want you back."

She shook her head, feeling misty and sad and unsure.

"Remember when we took that lost child back to her parents at the track yesterday?"

She nodded, unable to look at him, keeping her gaze firmly on the tasteful carpet in rusts and greens no doubt chosen by the Belgium-bound couple.

"That could have been us. It should have been us. It felt so right."

"But she wasn't ours. She was a child with her own family."

"Of course she wasn't ours. All I meant was that I looked over at you and I knew that we'd be great parents. We can have more kids," he said gently. "I want to have kids with you."

"If we can't get through one miscarriage without falling apart how will we ever manage to bring up children? What if they break their arms or get into the wrong crowd or take drugs or something?"

He'd moved closer without her even noticing, and now he put an arm around her and pulled her closer. "We'll figure it out as we go along. It's what everybody else does."

She wanted to pull away, but it felt so good in his arms. He kissed the top of her head and simply held her. "I wish I could believe you," she said at last. "But I'm scared that every time there's a problem you'll blow me off and go play poker or stay at work long hours or hide out in front of some TV somewhere."

"Then you'll have to haul my butt home, won't you?"

She'd never entirely accepted that she'd been at fault, too. But maybe she had.

"And when you turn into yourself and won't let me in, I'll have to stay right in your face until you talk about what's bothering you."

There was more to her hurt than that. He had to understand how she felt. "I know it wasn't anything but a one-in-five statistic to you, but to me it was a baby." She wiped her hand across her eyes. "I lost my dad and then I lost my baby within two weeks of each other. I feel like somehow it was my fault. If I hadn't got on that plane and stressed myself out going to see him, maybe things would have been different."

"I should have gone with you," he said. "Why didn't I? At least I would have been there for you."

"You had to work," she said, her voice gruff.

"I couldn't handle it. That's the truth. I didn't

know how to be around a guy in a coma. Can't joke him out of it, can't make anything better. I liked your dad a lot. I didn't want to see him like that. But it wasn't right to let you go there alone."

"And I didn't tell you how much I needed you to go with me."

"We were both wrong." He touched her hair gently, stroking the strands smooth. "If I could go back, I'd do things differently."

"You can never go back. That's the thing with time. It only goes in one direction."

"True, but you can learn from your mistakes, and we'd be different this time."

"How can you say that? We're still the same people."

"We're not, Tay. Look at us. We're sitting here talking about some tough stuff, and neither of us is running away. Don't you see? We have changed."

She sipped her tea, feeling that she needed to take some strength from the warm liquid. "Oh, I don't know. Maybe I made too much of a big deal about something that happens every day. You're right. One in five pregnancies does end in miscarriage. I guess I just got way ahead of myself." She pulled her feet up under her and curled into herself. "Remember when I bought that maternity top?" She shook her head. "I was nine weeks pregnant and buying a maternity top."

"You were picking out names, too."

She was about to argue but honesty stopped her. "How did you know that?"

"Sometimes you talk in your sleep."

"You never let on that you knew."

"I figured we'd call the kid after your dad. Andrew if it was a boy and Andrea if it was a girl."

"And you'd have been okay with that?"

"I didn't care what we called it. Didn't care if it was a boy or a girl, so long as…"

"So long as it was a healthy baby," she finished for him.

"Yeah."

In the silence she felt the beginning of hope stir. "Why didn't you ever talk to me then, about the baby?"

"I'm more about action than talking."

"Yeah. Running away from your problems being your best event." She faced him and said, "Turned out I was pretty good at that sport, too."

CHAPTER TWENTY-ONE

"HANG ON," HE SAID, RISING so abruptly her head fell back against the couch cushions.

"Where are you going?"

"I'll be right back."

She heard him pound upstairs and then she heard some strange sounds, like furniture being moved. What on earth?

After about ten minutes, when she'd finished her tea and wondered if she should go looking for him, she heard his steps thundering back down the stairway.

He was holding a box in his hand, about the size of a florist box but made of corrugated cardboard. He had the strangest look on his face. He was unsure of himself, she realized. It was so rare to see him like this.

"What's in the box?"

He thrust it toward her. "Open it."

She took the box, which was dusty on top and bore the logo of a custom-sports place in Seattle.

For some reason, she sat down before she opened it.

She lifted the lid and as she looked inside her heart broke all over again.

"Oh, Mike," she said.

Inside was a tiny baseball bat. There was script writing on the side she had to turn her head to read. It said, "Taylor-made."

She turned her head to find that Mike's face was a little crumpled. "It wasn't just a statistic to me."

She'd never seen him cry. She realized as she watched his eyes fill that she'd never seen him cry. She knew her own cheeks were wet as she threw herself into his arms and they held each other, giving and taking the comfort they hadn't been able to offer before when they'd both needed it so desperately.

She took the tiny baseball bat carefully out of the box and ran her finger over the script, which told her everything she needed to know.

She'd been so wrong. "I'm so sorry," she said. They talked far into the night. It seemed that once they'd started talking, they couldn't stop, sharing their pain and their foolishness in turning away from each other when their need was greatest.

"It was my fault for hiding at work so much," he said.

She shook her head. "It was my fault for running out on you. On us. I should have had more faith."

"I'm sorry."

"I'm sorry, too."

"I love you," he said.

"I love you, too," she echoed. "But I can't make any promises."

"Maybe this time, instead of rushing into a wedding, we should take some time."

She chuckled. "You think?"

"We'll go slowly. We'll see a counselor together."

"You'll hate that."

"Damn right, I will. But not as much as I would hate losing you again."

"Do we go public with this?"

He ran his fingers through her hair, one of those moves that always made her toes curl. "We could try it out on Dy and Kendall tomorrow." The pair had invited Mike and Taylor for an inaugural barbecue at their new house.

She turned and kissed him. "Perfect."

"And if they hate the idea, we'll definitely stop seeing each other," Mike said, kissing her back in a way that ended the conversation.

This time there was so much more than passion between them. There was forgiveness and hope, and the love they'd never quite given up on.

The following evening they parked and, avoiding the front door, walked around the side of the house hand in hand to where Dylan was fiddling with a shiny new barbecue and Kendall was reading the instruction manual.

"Why do I get the feeling dinner is going to be takeout?" Mike said.

"Hi," Taylor said.

Kendall put down the instruction manual and ran over to give both of them a big hug.

"You look totally blissed out," Taylor said, hugging her friend. The newlyweds had flown straight to the track from their honeymoon for the weekend's race, so this was the first time she'd really had a chance to see them.

"It was fantastic. I like this being married thing. Don't you, husband?"

Dylan rolled his eyes. Mike strolled over to help him figure out the new barbecue. Or at least to stand there and look manly.

"I can't help it. I keep calling him my husband. It's so juvenile, but I cannot seem to stop. I'd go into a store on some little island and say, 'Do you have any bottled water? My husband asked me to pick some up.'"

Taylor laughed. "You had a good time, then?"

"The best. The water is so amazingly blue. I've never seen—" She stopped, did a double take. "Wait a minute. When I first saw you two, were you holding hands?"

"You must still have sun blindness from sailing," Mike said.

Taylor glared at him. "We were holding hands." She shrugged. "New development."

Kendall's eyes widened. Dylan hid his surprise better, but not much better. "But you two hate each other."

They exchanged a glance. "It comes and goes."

Dylan smacked himself on the forehead. "She's the one, isn't she? Taylor's the one who had you quoting *Casablanca*."

It was Taylor's turn to look shocked. "You quoted *Casablanca* for me? I love that movie."

"Me, too," gushed Kendall. "Only I always want to change the ending so Humphrey Bogart and Ingrid Bergman get together."

"I know. It's so sad when they have to part."

Dylan seemed less interested in discussing the ending of *Casablanca* than in sorting through Mike's drunken ramblings to get at the truth. "You said something about a woman who wouldn't take your name. Who came back to kick you in the teeth a second time."

"Do you have to repeat the ravings of a drunk? I thought you were my friend."

"I thought you were mine. What have you been keeping from me? Did you know Taylor before she arrived in Charlotte?"

Mike walked over and took her hand again and squeezed. She squeezed back, letting him know it was okay to share whatever he wanted to share.

"We used to be married."

"You two?" Kendall asked, wide-eyed. "When? Where?"

"We got married almost five years ago. Lasted a little over three."

"We got divorced."

"I'm so sorry. Obviously the marriage was a mistake."

"No. The divorce was the mistake."

"Mike, we haven't completely decided yet."

Kendall put her hands over her mouth. "It must have been torture for you two when you found out you were standing in for us as the fake bride and groom."

"It wasn't so bad. That wedding got us talking again."

Dylan put an arm around his new wife and contemplated Mike and Taylor standing with their hands linked. "Taylor sure did look good in that first wedding dress she tried on in Charlotte."

"Dylan!"

"I'm just saying."

"I thought so, too," Mike said. "I'd never seen her look more beautiful."

"Wasn't your first wedding…?"

"We got married on a beach. It was a spur-of-the-moment thing."

"A spur-of-the-moment wedding?" Kendall looked as though she might pass out at the notion of a wedding that wasn't planned, coordinated and analyzed till death do us part.

"We'd do it differently if we did it again," Taylor said.

"*When* we do it again," Mike corrected.

"You know, I don't mean to boast, but I am an excellent wedding planner," Kendall said, linking arms with Taylor. "Seems a shame for those new skills to go to waste."

She looked at Mike, who was gazing at her a little the way Dylan was gazing at Kendall.

On impulse, she leaned over and kissed him. Something she planned to do a lot of in the days to come.

She knew they wouldn't rush into marriage the second time around, but she also knew that when it happened she'd be ready. She already had her dress picked out. She'd known it, too, when she modeled that gown for Kendall—oddly enough the first real wedding gown she'd ever tried on.

She had her venue all picked out, she realized, looking around her. Dy and Kendall's home would make a great spot for a wedding. And this time they'd invite all their friends and family and figure out what needed to be figured out.

The dinner was as much fun as dinner is when four people are all close friends and new love is in the air.

When they left at the end of the evening they drove back to Taylor's place.

"Would you like to come in?" she asked him.

"Yes, I would."

When they got to her place, she snapped on lights and put on some music.

She waited for him to kiss her, but he didn't. He gazed down at her for a moment and then said, "I bought you something today."

"Really? A present?"

He pulled out a small jeweler's box. A ring box. Her heart skittered. "Oh, Mike."

"Open it."

She opened the ring box and found a band of white gold with a ruby mounted in the center. Her birthstone. "It's gorgeous," she breathed.

"I found this great little jeweler uptown. One other thing we never had was an engagement ring. You can call this an engagement ring, or just an early birthday present if you prefer."

"What do you want it to be?" she asked.

"How about a promise ring? A symbol that we are starting over."

"That sounds like a good idea." No racing to the altar this time. They'd go slowly, take their time.

"I had it engraved."

She turned the ring sideways and squinted.

"Oh, Mike," she said, her words catching in her throat.

Inside the ring were engraved the words, *Turn Two.*

This time, they'd get it right.

Love Inspired

Celebrate Love Inspired's 10th anniversary with top authors and great stories all year long!

A Tiny Blessings Tale

Debra Watson's daughter, Mia, a new Christian, was beginning to feel at home in Chestnut Grove. And so was Debra, due to the charms of the small-town Christmas season…and those of attractive Christian Jonah Fraser. Could Debra get over her fears of love and finally settle down?

Look for

A Holiday To Remember

by Jillian Hart

Available December wherever you buy books.

Steeple Hill®

LI87460